FIRST COMES
Love

DELYSE CLAYDEN

BALBOA.
PRESS

A DIVISION OF HAY HOUSE

Balboa Press books may be ordered through booksellers or by contacting:

Balboa Press
A Division of Hay House
1663 Liberty Drive
Bloomington, IN 47403
www.balboapress.com.au
1 (877) 407-4847

Print information available on the last page.

ISBN: 978-1-5043-1661-3 (sc)
ISBN: 978-1-5043-1662-0 (e)

Balboa Press rev. date: 02/21/2019

DEDICATION:

To my family, who provide the drama, humour and love that I write about. Especially my husband Roo, who helps me feel beautiful xxx

ACKNOWLEDGEMENTS:

My first acknowledgement is to my son Ethan, for basically daring me to try to publish my book! By trying to be a good role model for you, you have actually inspired me! Thank you for encouraging me to give life a go.

My Mum, Debra, thank you for being the kind of Mum that encourages me to live my dreams. You have the biggest heart of anyone I know, and the first critic and sounding board for my ideas. You also help care for the kids so I can write, so you need a lot of credit!

To the L Club ladies, my friends Sarah, Janine, Rachel and Alicia for reading it, liking it, and asking for more! Thank you for being honest, and spending time helping me and listening to many hours of talk about it. Oh, and thank you for the research ideas and parties!

An especially big thanks to Rachel for helping me to edit, and the funny comments in the margins about the steamy parts! I feel very blessed to have people like you ladies around.

To Regina and Tori Rash, thank you so much for being my USA contacts, and helping me get my drafts. You are very kind, and I am glad you enjoyed the book.

And, to my friend Azza Aly and your team. You are literally the most amazing woman I have ever met. Determined, kind, very funny and kick-ass! Thank you for stepping up and making the world a better place. Anne for PM!

:-Dee xxx

CHAPTER 1

"Fuuuuckkkkk!"

That was the first thing Beth thought when she opened her eyes on Monday morning. 9:15 am and she was already late, with a hangover the size of Australia. She couldn't believe they did it to her again. Time for some new friends she decided. First day of second semester and Beth was determined to do better this time round. As she looked across the room at her best friend, who was passed out on her white on white bed linen, Beth wondered if Lori had ever had a bad hair day in her life. Not since she had known her. And considering they met when they were three, Beth was used to the differences in the two of them. Used to it was a lot different with being ok with it though.

Let's face it, her best friend was stunning. Slim, beautiful, long dark hair. Legs all the way to Christmas. And the shitty thing too, was that she was smart to go with it. Dux of their Primary school in year seven. Pretty hard on your self-esteem when your best friend is a 10 and you would struggle to call yourself a 5. Beth always knew they were different, but lately, those differences were making her feel like an ugly step sister. Have you seen that movie "DUFF"? That's how Beth saw herself, and up until last year, she was ok with being the designated ugly fat friend. Blonde with a dash of purple highlights, medium height, overweight and of average intelligence. Her best asset was the decent size boobs that adorned her chest. And she had them way before everyone else, so for a while she got a bit of attention. But now? Beth was beginning to think of herself as almost invisible to the male population. When she thought about it, Beth knew that this lack of attention was the real reason for her green-eyed monster glance at her roommate. What does a girl have to do to get a boy to look at her? Scratch that she reminded herself. You're eighteen now, you need a man. And you need him to do a lot more than look.

Just as Beth decided the hangover from last night was not going anywhere, best friend number two, aka Matthew James, rolled over. Puttting his arm over her, Matthew pulled her back into the bed. It always amazed her how Matthew ended up stealing the covers from her, and not her perfectly formed roommate. Rolling over to look at him, Beth thought about the first time she met Matthew. Belmay Kindergarten, day one, and Beth walked up to the group of boys kicking a ball. Asking for a turn, Beth liked sports even at a young age. Matthew, the closest to the ball, picked up the footy and told her that girls can't kick a footy. With that, he walked away. So Beth did what any self-respecting young lady would do. She ran and tackled him, grabbed the ball and kicked as far as she could, over the fence and out of the playground. Teaching that chauvinist four year old an important lesson. They had been friends ever since. Lori wasn't too keen on letting a boy into their cubby house at first, but soon Lori realised how useful it was to have him around. The girls always used him to fix the cubby, climb on the roof to get the ball and carry the sleeping bags when they had sleep overs. Beth liked that she could muck around with him and get dirty, but still play Barbies with Lori. And now they had a Daddy for their games of families. Except when Lori made him be the dog or the grumpy grandad.

Matthew James was another 10 on the scale for hotness. His wavy dark curls, always a little too long, fell loosely over his face. Although they were closed now, Beth pictured his bright green eyes and brushed his hair away from his face. The slow, handsome smile that appeared made the dimple in his left cheek sink into his scruffy unshaved cheek. Tanned, muscular and oh boy did he know it sexy, Matthew had developed into model good looks.

"Morning Bee" Matthew whispered as he opened his eyes and flashed the green jewels at Beth.

Beth stopped playing with his hair and reached for the sheet to cover her underwear only clad body. He couldn't help it, Matthew grabbed the sheet and had a good hard look at her chest. And got hit in the head with a pillow for his efforts.

"Morning shit head" Beth replied, only half meaning it.

"What did I do this time?" he asked, knowing his best friend wasn't serious. "You know I love it when you talk dirty to me" he said with a devilish smirk.

"Really Hue? You keep me up all night partying because you couldn't bare to go without me, steal my covers all night and then get a morning eye-full of my tits. All while making me late for my first class. So much for me turning over a new leaf this semester."

Beth moved so she could get off the bed gracefully, taking the sheet to cover herself. Matthew pulled on her arm,

"Come back Bee and play with my hair again, you know I love it." Matthew begged.

Beth ramped up the strength and took her arm and her purple sheet away from the bed. Well wasn't that fine and dandy, because this left a finely toned Matthew in a pair of snug fitting jocks, lying seductively on her bed. Good morning six pack! Beth looked away. She had seen his body enough to know how hot he was. And how modest he was not. Really, it was like living with Ken and Barbie.

Except Ken and Barbie in this dolls house never hooked up. Beth wondered, not for the first time, why Lori and Matthew had never been together. Talk about the genetic lottery if they ever reproduced. But as far as Beth knew, neither of her best friends had seen each other like that. They both had had enough partners to work out preferences by now. And after fourteen years of friendship, if it was going to happen, you'd probably think it would have. The fact is, the three of them had been almost like siblings their entire lives. Beth rushed to her wardrobe and just grabbed the first thing she found and raced to the bathroom before Matthew had time to comment again. Just as she was turning on the shower, there was a knock on the door.

"Bethy, baby, I need to pee, let me in" Matthew mumbled through the door.

"Use the sink I'm naked in here!" Beth sighed in exasperation.

"I won't look I promise Bee. Come on, I need to drain it."

Wrapping the towel around herself, Beth unlocked the door and stepped back, covering as much of her body as she could. No one had ever seen her naked, and even though her best friend always joked about her gorgeous curves and boobs, Beth assumed it was his attempt to make her feel good. If he actually saw her body, he wouldn't joke. Cursing her Double D cups and her flabby tummy, Beth was a realist. Landing a 10 like Matthew was one of those Rom/Com deals. So far out of reality, even Hollywood cringes.

Waiting outside the bathroom door, Beth's mind wandered to thoughts about finally losing her virginity. Someone would eventually see her naked body. Would she keep the light on? No. No need to scare them off too quickly. Let's face it, at this point, she was not holding out for true love. A mild interest would be enough. Just to see what all the fuss was about. She just needed to find someone as desperate as she was. Lack of sleep was making her horny she reasoned.

As Matthew stepped out of the bathroom, his cheeky smile made Beth blush. She couldn't help it, he really was good to look at.

"Need me to wash your back darling?" Matthew said with that infuriating clever lift of a single eyebrow.

Annnnd there was the mouth that snapped her back to reality.

"You wouldn't know what to do with all this woman Hue" Beth said gesturing to herself as she shoved him out the way, hard.

"But oh it would be fun learning!" she heard him shout as she closed the door.

Got to hand it to him, the boy was smooth. Beth chuckled as she stepped under the steaming water. Would she find a man that would make her laugh like her best friend did? She couldn't imagine finding someone to talk to and muck around with as good as him. They had a perfect relationship. They liked the same sports, movies, mostly music and talked for hours about everything. Beth actually felt closer to Matthew than Lori sometimes. She always considered herself a tomboy rather than a girlie girl. How awesome could life be with an orgasm or two thrown in?

"Shit, make this quick" Beth thought to herself as she soaped up her body and dreamed of strong hands moving their way down. Was there an equivalent to 'Blue Balls' for women? She was going a little cuckoo with desperation and horniness. Brushing her teeth and throwing on some moisturizer were the only real steps Beth had in her beauty regime. Makeup was not her priority like it was for Lori. Beth could never understand it, because she had always seen Lori as a natural beauty, no need to cover it.

As Beth stepped out of the bathroom, BFF eye candy was dressed and sitting at the table reading a book. A steaming cup of tea sitting in front of him, the human anatomy book pages being scanned and turned at a steady pace. Brains not just beauty Beth thought. No time to enjoy the view though, she was late.

"See ya babe" Beth called as she kissed him on the cheek and picked up her satchel.

"Wait, Beth, I made you a cuppa to take with you."

Beth stepped back from the door and smiled. Matthew held out her favourite purple travel mug, and two Panadol.

"What would I do without you Hue?" Beth murmured taking the precious gifts and flashing a full-face grin. "Probably not get hungover and late in the first place?" Matthew answered returning the smile.

"Love you, have a great day" Beth said with a chuckle as she raced out the door.

She was half way to her car when she heard a whistle and looked up. Matthew was leaning out the window from the second story apartment. Pulling his arm back, he released a paper aeroplane that sailed in a perfect arc and landed just two steps away from her. She opened it up. This had always been their preferred methods of communication throughout school. They got very good at aiming. The messy boy writing read "Love you too, call me about dinner tonight". Beth warmed at the message and looked up. He really was sweet. Giving a nod she turned and raced for her car.

Driving the few streets away to get to Uni, Beth wondered if Lori was even up yet. "Let her sleep" she thought. Lori had been partying hard and studying hard lately. Beth had the worrying feeling that something was wrong. Nothing overtly obvious, just the intensity of her friend had kicked up a notch, and boy that was saying something. Lori had always been the graceful, effortlessly sophisticated one, with an air of mystery about her. She was the epitome of playing hard to get. Most men saw her as a sought after prize. Most woman thought of her as a cold hearted bitch. Yes, she was somewhat moody to people she didn't know, but mostly it was simply because she was smarter than everyone else, and had a low bullshit tolerance. If Lori was a man, people would call her strong, determined and a leader. But as a young woman, she was judged by her stunning looks rather than her sharp intellect. Beth had always been in awe of her best friend. Proud, her number one fan, and always pinching herself that she got to be the one living across the road from the most popular girl in school, Beth adored Lori for many years, and probably, if she was honest, still did. Shaking her head to clear out of the reverie, Beth geared up for another late walk in to hard arses' lecture.

CHAPTER 2

Watching Beth drive away, Matthew had no desire to go home. What was waiting for him there? An empty house with too many undone chores and a drunk Step-Dad that may or may not be off the couch. Staying with Beth was his real home. He even tolerated Lori in small doses, but since they were young, if he wanted time with Beth, he had to put up with her royal highness too. He couldn't see why all his mates wanted to hook up with her. Too high maintenance for him. Besides, he preferred blondes.

Matthew stepped back from the window and glanced at the messy, multi-coloured bed he considered shared property. "That girl and her bright colours" he thought. Yep, the two sides of the bedroom were strikingly different. The blah, blah boring white on Lori's side, and the warm, welcoming rainbow on his side. Oops, Beth's side. It was just too easy to consider it his as well. The girls had only moved into the apartment 6 months ago, but the 40 minute drive to stay here and see his best friend was no hassle at all. If they would stop being stubborn and let him use the spare room life would be much easier. Never going to his official address, and living with Beth would be fine with him.

When moving in, the girls came up with a great plan to share the biggest room that lead directly into the shared living/kitchen area, and turn the other tiny room into a study. Beth's solution to the "I don't want to let Lori have the huge room" problem. Matthew had backed her all the way. Princess Lori needed a lot of convincing but eventually she caved. Even she could see the benefit of having a quiet place to study. Matthew had been so proud of his girl for standing her ground for a change. She was too nice to everyone, and always put others before herself. That was one of the things he loved about her. Not that she was a push over by any means. Especially not with him. When something was really important to Beth, she didn't stop until justice was served, wrongs were righted and all was fair in her world again. Man he was lucky to have a friend like her. She really did make others feel good about themselves and Matthew was determined to ensure others did the same for her. Including her temperamental roommate.

Finding the wayward sheet, Matthew made the bed, and decided leaving was going to have to happen soon. It felt too empty right now without his Bethany. With class not until 1pm, maybe he would go and study at the library. Brushing his teeth and putting his tooth brush back in its normal spot next to Beth's, Matthew gave his face a quick splash of water and moved quietly through the apartment hoping to avoid Lori altogether. Three steps from the door, a snarling comment came at him from the corner.

"Best view of you there is Hue, watching you leave."

Taking a deep breath, Matthew decided to be the bigger person and let it slide. As he turned to shut the door though, he couldn't help himself. He flipped Lori the bird as she threw dagger eyes at him. He chuckled loudly as he left the building, knowing how much that would have pissed her off.

You know, he hadn't minded her for all these fourteen years. Up until last year he actually considered her a friend. They knew the same people, and she was handy having friends that he could hook up with. Things were different now though. And they would never be the same. Late last year, Matthew had heard Lori joking in front of her minions that her best friend was the best devoted slave there was. They all joked about Beth behind her back and it made Matthew's blood boil. Lori even tried to persuade him to take her to the Year 12 ball despite knowing he was going with Beth. Her comment?

"Why would you settle for second prize when you can have number one?"

Matthew had never hit a girl, but bloody hell he was close to it that night. He kept that secret buried from Beth, knowing it would devastate her. She idolised Lori for some unknown reason. Always wanted to be like her. Completely unnecessary in Matthews' eyes. The world needed more Beth's, with her welcoming smile, quirky sense of humour and enthusiasm for life. One Lori was more than anyone needed.

Deciding to walk the short distance, leaving his car where it was, Matthew was hoping to clear his still foggy brain. He plugged in his headphones and blasted some Cold Chisel to improve his mood. Seven more hours and he would be calm again. His best friend did that to him, and lately he really needed it. With work being flat out, and home life sucking balls, even the buffet of leggy blondes throwing themselves at him this year had not improved the situation. In fact it seemed to be making it worse. Hollow, meaningless sex with cookie cutter, nothing between the ears bombshells was great in theory. In practice it was actually boring. How did so many clueless girls actually make the grades to get into uni he wondered.

Finding a hook-up was always easy for Matthew. Girls had always thrown themselves at him. This was how he knew he was ok in the looks department. And he learnt it at an early age. Using his naturally toned body, he found it easy to get in the pants of every girl he ever wanted. Benefit of playing endless sports and being good at it. Never needed to Jack up in the gym. Matthew even knew the affect he had on the female staff anywhere he went. A nurses' pass to leave school early, sure thing Mr James. All it took was a small smile and a wink. Last year, even the new drama teacher, fresh graduate with acting dreams was infatuated with him. The leading male role in the school production was the result, thank you very much. The bonus was that he had practice with Beth three times a week, so more excuses not to go to where his 'rents lived.

Breakfast at Sweethearts switching to Khe Sahn, Beth's favourite duo with him, Matthew found himself singing his parts out loud, as he made it to the sprawling Mt Lawley ECU campus. Matthew was studying physiotherapy, with dreams of working with top athletes one day. A talented cricketer and football player himself, Matthew "speedy" James had pace and stamina on his side. Perhaps if he had a different upbringing, supportive home life, he may have made it big. The fact that his local Belmont clubs had all let him play for free since he was nine years old, was an indicator on how good he was. They wanted him badly. The truth was, Beth had always been the only source of support in Matthew's life. His strength, self-belief and interest in the world was all due to the girl with the purple hair and beautiful smile. With his mum always working to support his no good older brother and lazy step dad, he had spent most of his life as a key latch kid, with his family having no idea where he was, what he did or even if he ate. He never knew his real dad. Terry, his older brother says he had met him a few times, but apparently, their mum had a taste for useless men because he shot through when Matthew was 1 and hasn't been seen since.

Finding a cubicle in the silent study area, Matthew took out his text books and threw himself into making this Uni thing work. He was determined to lift himself out of the coupon and Good Sammy status that had plagued him so far in his life. Beth had always told him he could achieve anything and he really wanted to prove her right. He still needed to convince himself though. This scholarship was his only chance to make Beth proud. What was with him today? Every thought came back to his best friend. Was he getting too dependent on her? Shit that ship had sailed about 10 years ago. "Focus dude" he chided himself and got back to taking notes. An image of his best friend next to him in bed this morning floated into his brain causing him to drop his pen and blink. OK, not going there. Yes he loved her. She was the best and only thing in his life. The explicit thoughts running through his head right now was not what a girl like her deserved and Matthew put a mental road block up. Adjusting his pants so he sat a little more comfortably with the sudden tightness in his groin area, Matthew resumed his exploration of muscle groups and human anatomy and pushed his sudden urge aside.

Three hours later he was still rock hard and sitting uncomfortably in the lecture theatre prowling for something or someone, to ease the building pressure down below. This wasn't the first-time thoughts of Bethany had made him hard, but for some reason today, it wasn't going away. Bingo, Matthew thought, pretty blonde at six o'clock swinging her hair and looking at him. What was her name again? Fuck it, doesn't matter, he was so jacked he couldn't care less. In between the lecture and the tutorial he would find a quiet place to take her. Let's hope she wasn't a clinger though. What he needed right now was to diffuse the bomb in his pants so he could be on an even keel when he saw Beth for dinner tonight. Shit. Back to her. No. As his pants twitched again he turned to the blonde and smiled. Her responding smile should have caused a surge in the power its wattage was so big. Too easy, he thought as he shifted a few seats over and ramped up the charm.

CHAPTER 3

Slipping into the back of the lecture theatre, Beth managed to avoid eye contact with Professor Hammond. Brilliant, inspiring, but deadly serious, this was a teacher who knew her stuff. And Beth was learning so much. Early Childhood was definitely what she wanted to teach. She had an affinity with small children. And to be the best you had to learn from the best. Looking slowly to her left, Beth noticed another late comer slip in next to her. Beth flashed the girl a knowing grin and got ready to take notes. Late comer quietly coughed and then cursed. Beth glanced sideways again and saw the laggie had tears in her eyes.

Moving closer, Beth held out a tissue and quietly introduced herself.

"Hi, I'm Bethany Holden. Can I help at all?"

Beth could now see into those pretty blue eyes and delicate features. The girl smiled weakly through her tears.

"Hi, I'm Jo. Joanna. Thanks for the tissue. I can't believe I forgot a pen. It really hasn't been the best start to the day."

Offering Joanna a spare pen, Beth could sympathise.

"Honestly, me either, I got here about thirty seconds before you." Beth admitted with a wry smile.

Jo looked up from her now wet tissue and smiled. A real, no faking it, smile. Wow, this girl was too adorable Beth thought.

"I don't feel like such a loser myself now, thank you." Said Jo with a grin as she took out her notebook and started jotting things down.

Beth giggled and as the two began focussing on the lecture in front of them, a silent bond formed. Sitting with Jo in the tutorial afterwards, Beth enjoyed meeting new people and sharing opinions and thoughts. Last semester, Beth felt she had been too preoccupied with just keeping her head above water to make anything more than wave hello friends. It felt good to relate to someone a bit deeper. And they seemed to have a lot in common. The only difference for Jo was that she was all on her own. Having just moved from Sydney, being an only child and her parents having passed away in a car crash, Jo had no one. An obscure Uncle she had only met once, was her sole reason for coming West. Her cousin, a year older than Jo, was meant to call her three weeks ago, and she still hadn't met him. Beth felt so lucky to have both her best friends at the same Uni as her, and she was close to her Mum and Dad too. The universe was smiling on Jo that day Beth thought. She was the perfect friend for Jo, and knew her friends would be supportive too.

When Professor Hammond walked into the class, she looked straight at Beth and said "Glad you could make it on time Miss Holden. Sorry my 9am lecture is too early for you. Maybe you need to find another lecture that won't cut into your social life too much."

Beth flushed at the unwanted attention. Obviously, she wasn't as subtle as she thought she was earlier arriving late. The woman in front of her may be brilliant, but man she was tough.

"I am very sorry professor, I have been unwell recently, but I am feeling much better now." Beth spluttered.

"I see, well, you have great potential and natural teaching ability, so I hope I am not wasting my time with you. You need to step up a gear from last semester. See that it happens."

"Will do, I promise." Beth replied completely flabbergasted at the dressing down.

Wait, there was a compliment in there somewhere too wasn't there?

Jo, sitting quietly next to her, let out a long breath and Beth realised she needed to do the same. In their shared exhale, the girls started laughing quietly. The rest of the tute was smooth sailing with Beth being her normal inquisitive self. She always worried what the other classmates thought of her putting her hand up to ask questions all the time. At lunch in the cafeteria, Beth decided to ask Jo.

"So, you know how I can get a little pushy with asking questions in class? I was wondering, does anyone ever say anything? Like, am I the MOST annoying person in the class or what?"

"Not the MOST annoying," Jo giggled but added, "that girl with the flannel shirt and hairy legs, who always asks about how come we can't bring corporal punishment back takes the number one spot. You would just be a close second."

"Ha, well, I feel so much better now!"

"Seriously though Beth, I love that you ask questions, most of the time you have the courage to ask things I never would. And it is all important stuff. You ask things I never would have thought to care about."

"Thanks Jo, I do worry what the others think of me, and besides, you are my only new friend this year. My roommate is studying Psychology and my other best friend is learning to be a physio. They don't exactly understand my desire to teach."

"I see you talking to everybody. What about that girl that said hello to you five minutes ago?"

"Well, I don't even remember her name, I do remember she had a younger sister named Emily though. She has Autism and we were talking about how Emily wanted to study special needs teaching to learn how to help."

"You are amazing. I wish I could make friends as easy as you" Jo said, already feeling happy at having someone as thoughtful as Beth to talk to. Best thing that had happened to her in a long time.

When it was time to move on to their next classes, Beth wasn't ready to say goodbye. Sending Matthew and Lori a quick text, she asked Jo to join them for dinner that night at the local pizza place. The sparkle in the girls eyes was enough of a clue to Beth that she had made the right decision. This girl needed a new family, and she was the perfect person to give it to her. Hey, maybe even Matthew and Jo would hit it off? He did like blondes. As her stomach swirled with a strange feeling, Beth waved goodbye to her new friend and continued on to art. This was one of her favourite specialisation areas, and today they were starting a theme based programme. Beth had already decided she would do her whole theme on Frogs. Something about all the different shaded greens she could use made her happy. It also reminded her of Matthew and how they would spend hours outside playing footy and cricket. She loved watching him bowl, and she wasn't too bad herself. Green was definitely a happy colour for Beth, and this art unit was going to be awesome.

Beths phone beeped with a message from Lori,

"No problem, got a new lost puppy?"

Oh boy, so Lori's hangover was bad too Beth was guessing.

"Will fill you in L8R, she is nice. Love ya, hv a GR8 Day xxx"

Matthew messaged just as Beth reached the lecture door, on time – hooray!

"No worries, is she hot?"

Grrrrr, really Matthew? But this is what she had thought herself initially right? He didn't need to be a pig about it though. Jo needed a support group, not a strip tease.

"Behave stud. This girl needs friends. :-P" was the reply she sent.

Maybe this wasn't such a good idea. Oh well, too late now, she thought pulling on her apron and finding a space at the art counter. The professor was always late, and didn't care less what happened as long as you turned in your work on time. All part of the process he believed. You can't rush inspiration. Beth loved both these approaches to teaching and thought she herself was somewhere in the middle of 'don't rush inspiration' and 'strive to achieve more'.

Waiting, Beth found herself thinking of her best friends and how different they were. She was starting to feel a drift between the three of them, and longed for the days when it was the three of them against the world. The complications of growing up were changing things.

She herself was very different now, so her friendship would definitely be changing. Beth cringed at the twelve year old version of herself that had the biggest crush on Matthew. This was the first tingle of attraction to boys she had had, and he was always around, so it felt natural to crush on him. It had taken approximately twelve months of convincing herself that he would never love her like that before she actually had a boyfriend. Ben was a shy, but sweet boy who obviously used all his courage to ask her out. Matthew hated him. But Beth was just happy to have some attention, even if the poor boy was too shy to make a move. In the end she dumped him for lack of action and moved on to Adam, an Italian Stallion with a reputation and dark good looks.

If Matthew had disliked Ben, then he hated Adam with a passion. The boys did not get on well, and the three months that she dated Adam, she had to keep them separate. When Adam dumped her, Beth was glad to be away from the saliva soaking when they kissed, and the fact that she could see her friend a bit more eased the blow of being dumped. But it still hurt when Adam told everyone that Beth was frigid and didn't let him do anything. She was only fourteen! Matthew didn't take that well either, and when Adam returned to school after a week off, he was still sporting a few bruises on his face. Beth never had the courage to ask Matthew if he did it, but in her heart she knew. Man he was good to her. She really hoped he would find someone to care for him like he deserved. God only knew his family was useless. Practically non –existent in his life. Beth wondered what was with her today. She couldn't shake her thoughts away from Matthew. His cheeky glance at her chest and offer to wash her in the shower had warmed her lady parts. Time to reality check girl, she thought. He sees you as a friend, possibly a sister. As if on a cue from her chaotic mind, crazy Prof. Cooper strolled in. With his polka dot bow tie and paint splattered slacks, his appearance threw Beth a lifeline, distracting her from her aching libido.

CHAPTER 4

Lori saw red as the no good bludger left the flat. No doubt he would be back tonight. She really wished he had his own place to go. Hadn't all these years been enough for her to put up with him? And his puppy dog glances at Beth made her skin crawl. Every other boy had wanted her. She was always on the top of the TO DO list for every boy she met except Matthew James. What was his problem? He couldn't seriously be in love with Beth could he? Shit. That was it hey? That's the real reason he turned her down last year right? She loved her best friend, probably more than she would ever admit, but for the life of her couldn't understand how Beth always made loads of friends and kept going with the warm and fuzzies. Don't get her wrong, Beth was the best sort of person, caring, always helping others. But on the looks side, she didn't have the IT factor that Lori did. It didn't make sense.

Slowly walking around the apartment, Lori tried to pull herself out of the grumps before she ruined her whole day. No classes meant she should really be focussing on her readings and getting ahead. This course was kicking her arse, a fact she was not ready to admit to anyone. Lori couldn't understand what had changed. She always got excellent grades. The last six months here? Lori felt herself slip into mediocrity and she did not like it one bit.

Her whole life, Lori had been the centre of attention. Always being praised for how beautiful she was, and how good at running she had become. It was easy to appear smart in school because the teachers always graded her up. She even tested the theory that she could do no wrong, when she submitted the exact same homework as Beth. Her best friend was given 7/10 while Lori was given 10/10 on the exact same questions. Apparently she was allowed some interpretation room, while her friend was not. What was with that? Lori had grown to hate her favouritism. How would she ever know if she was really good enough? Strict Italian parents had ruled her life so much that she now had an intrinsic need to excel. Never allowed to do any after school activities unless it was academic, Lori took up running as an excuse to get out of the house. Her dad had been putty in her hands for once, when she told him it was so she could keep her figure. She was 10 years old. Never allowed to cut her long hair, or eat unhealthy, her Nazi father controlled everything, because his daughter was to be smart and thin, with long hair and focussed on family above all else.

He couldn't control her at school though, so Lori rebelled out of sight of her family. Flirting, wearing makeup, rolling her supposedly long skirt up to flash-you length, Lori ramped up the sex appeal that seemed to make people notice. But she never let anyone close. This was just an image after all. In reality, she was a scared little girl. The only person who knew what life was like for Lori was Beth. She had seen it. She had mopped up the tears Lori shed over her punishment of two weeks solitary confinement for having a second dessert of apple pie. Two weeks with no school and being confined to her bedroom because she wanted more food. It broke her heart because it was the faction carnival and interschool carnival weeks she missed. Her running events, that made her feel fearless and free, had been stolen from her. When that man punished her, he really knew how to cut her down to nothing.

Enter the alter ego. No one would ever see her show emotion like that again. Beth was different. Beth would hold onto that for her and be the only one who truly saw her. So what, if people called her a snob, or that the jealous girls at school called her a bitch. She was smart, thin and desired by the male population. The ice cool mask was like her armour. Knowing when to turn on the charm, for the adults, and when to play hard to get for the boys was entirely due to her quick intellect. Lori read people easy. Human facial expressions, mannerisms and body language had always fascinated Lori, so going into a psych degree seemed ideal. The only trouble so far, these teachers actually marked her fairly. No more favouritism. After all this time, the thing that disgusted her originally, actually scared her now. What if it was too late? What if all she had thought of herself, the package she thought she was, was now equivalent to nothing?

Making herself a black coffee, Lori waded into the study and booted up the Mac. A few hours of reading and she would go for a run. She would talk to Beth about it tonight if Matthew ever left them alone. Two readings down and feeling good, a text came through from Beth. Great, a new lost soul Beth was trying to save. Sending her a quick reply, Lori sighed and thought about all they had been through together. Beth really was the best kind of person there was and truth be told, Lori did not like having to share her. Considering all the tragedy in her life, Beth was strong, giving and always seemed fucking happy. Where the hell did the girl get her cheery from? And the girl always came out of things better than she was before. Friends flocked to her, she was coming into her own with good grades this year and she had parents that actually liked her the way she was. Time for a run Lori thought before she slipped into a pity party again.

Changing into some lycra pants and a crop top, Lori pounded the pavement around their modest Mt Lawley home listening to Pink! Telling her to 'Try'. It was a nice area, only a small distance from the Uni and Lori had to admit again, that Beth was good for finding this place. The freedom that came with moving out of a controlling home and in with her best friend, was exhilarating. They had partied hard and eaten whatever they liked. And Lori had practically cut off contact with her parents. Paying for the apartment and her lifestyle meant getting a job fast. And the sports store five km's away hired her even before they saw her resume'. To them, it was important that she looked good in the products. The fact that she had more than air between the ears was just a bonus they hadn't expected. After the initial dumbed down run through, and treating her like she might faint if she was given too much to do, Lori had exceeded their expectations, bringing in new customers, and giving the store a thorough leap into the new century.

Circling back to the place she felt more at home at than she ever had, Lori stretched into some warm downs, and returned to her sanctuary. Making her way to the bathroom, Lori suddenly felt the urge to be quicker, as she ungracefully emptied her stomach contents in the porcelain throne. Not this again she thought to herself, wondering why this was the fifth day in a row with the oral pyrotechnics. She had only a small hangover this morning, nothing she wasn't used to, so surely they can't be related. Definitely time for a shower now, and standing under the warm pressure made her feel a whole lot better. Suck it up Princess she thought to herself as she dressed in some fresh clothes and blow dried her dark hair. Back to the readings she decided until Beth got home and they went to dinner. Maybe they would have time to talk before they left.

CHAPTER 5

Beth left her last class for the day feeling good. It was nice to find something you were actually good at for a change. She was used to being the average Annie, so the shock of doing well still surprised her regularly. Waving to some girls she knew from last semester, Beth tried to shift her thinking away from her best friends, but something was nagging at her. Lori had been distant – even with her, and Beth was the only one that knew the nice inside of Lori. It was like she was shutting her out. Had something happened? Was it that twenty five year old she was dating a few weeks ago? No relationship had ever left her like this. She was always in control. Since they were kids, Lori had the shield up. Man her parents had screwed her up. While other kids were playing on the street and sharing lollies with their friends, Lori was holed up in her room reading Shakespeare and chemistry text books. It didn't matter that none of it interested her. This is what filled Beth's thoughts as did pictures of Matthew. Let's not think about him again she reminded herself. In the short distance to her car and along the road to home, Beth made up her mind to actively seek out a boyfriend before the end of the year. She couldn't go on only thinking about Matthew. Her daily walks were not doing shit to her flabby body Beth lamented. Time to ask Lori for some tips and take up running if she wanted to succeed.

It wasn't as if Beth wasn't fit. In fact, her ability to play just about any sport was amazing compared to Lori, who stuck to running and

"Didn't do group sports". Netball, cricket, footy, hockey, Beth had played them all with varied success. Her favourite past time was cricket though, but the girls' team had folded due to lack of players. The last season she spent her time watching Matthew and helping his team at training. She knew all the team well, and they treated her as one of the boys. Jokes about her helping to fit their box in, and requests for groin massages aside, she knew they didn't see her as a potential lay. Beth was going to have to expand her pool of males if she wanted to lose her virginity any time soon.

Finally home, Beth entered the apartment to silence. Leaving her keys in the bowl near the door, and dropping her satchel, Beth walked into the bedroom she shared with her best friend, to find Lori asleep in an uncomfortable ball. Very unlike her girl to have a nap. Beth picked out a nice black and purple flowered dress and made her way quietly to the shower. Today she needed to soak the leftover alcohol out of her body and ease her worried heart under the warm spray. Taking time to blow dry her hair, Beth dawdled in the bathroom, even applying a coat of lipstick. Time to start making an effort if she wanted a man she decided. Moving into the kitchen Beth noticed it was already five O'clock and Lori needed to wake up. They had all had a late night, but something about this nap had alarm bells ringing.

Beth approached the bed where her friend was laying, and quietly spoke her name.

"Lolly. Lolly, time to wake up sweet thing".

With a groan, Lori opened her eyes and took a good two minutes to orientate herself. As Beth looked down at her friend, she noticed the dark circles under her eyes and the grey look to her skin. Apparently goddesses could get hangovers she thought.

"You look terrible Lolly. I won't ask if you are ok, cos clearly you are not. What can I do sweetheart?" Beth asked as she lowered herself down next to the bed and stroked the girl's long hair.

"I'm ok Bee. Just taking a bit longer to shake this hangover I think. I could do with a cuppa if you're offering." Lori said still groggy.

Beth looked closely at her friend. Suspecting Lori was trying to be tough, she played along with nonchalance as she said, "No worries babe, I will cancel, we can stay in and I will fuss over you. Not that you deserve it, you were part of my reason for being late this morning. How do I let you two talk me into things?"

Lori barked a sharp reply,

"Don't you dare blame me, try your lover boy. God knows he can't do anything without you."

Ouch! Even though Beth could admit it seemed that way, her outburst hurt.

"Wow! Ouch! And you know very well Matthew isn't my lover boy. What is with you lately? Why all the hate on Hue? I am starting to really worry about you darling."

Beth had already turned towards the kitchen when Lori spoke again,

"You know what, forget the tea, you go play families with your boy and your new project. I think I'd prefer my own company tonight."

With a sigh, Beth faced her friend and felt miles away from where she wanted to be.

"You don't mean that Lolly. I will stay with you, you are important to me, and no matter how shitty you try to be to me, you're not getting rid of me. So, deal OK?"

Lori almost smiled. Yep, her selfless friend would do that too. No way was she having that on her conscience thanks.

"No seriously, I just want to crash. Look, you did your hair and everything. Don't waste all that effort. I am just shitty from the hangover and stressed about study. A solitary night in will do me good."

Beth was torn. She really shouldn't leave. But she really did want to go out tonight. She contemplated her options and after a moment said, "Ok, well the deal is, I will go, see Jo and Hue and then I will bring you home some soup from the Chinese place on the corner. Then I will plait your hair and paint your nails. We will snuggle up and fall asleep watching crappy TV. OK?"

"Sounds like a plan." Replied Lori.

"Good. Well sit tight, I will see you soon." Beth left the apartment still worried but happy to have a plan of action.

Just a quick bite to eat, and she would return and give her friend the third degree about what the hell was going on. Throw in some pamper time and hopefully she would get answers. Nearly to her car, Beth heard a whistle and saw Matthew close his car door. Man did he look good leaning against his car like he owned the world.

"Well, look at you. What is the occasion sweet pea?" Matthew purred.

"What, just because I brushed my hair, you think there has to be an occasion? Can't a girl do anything? I can't live my whole life with you being the only man in my bed. Time I broadened my horizons Hue. Time for a whole new me if I am ever going to get anyone interested in me. I mean, what's a girl got to do to get laid?" Beth rambled a little too forcefully.

Choking a little, Matthew took a step towards Beth and opened his arms wide. Beth instantly threw herself at her friend and accepted the strong arms around her.

"What the hell are you talking about now crazy one? You're beautiful. No, don't argue." Matthew said as he pulled back to look her in the eyes.

It killed him to hear her say she needed to change. That would rip him apart. This was a girl who was already perfect.

"Listen, I don't know what has you flipping out like this, but believe me, you are fine the way you are. Any man would be lucky to have you. Besides, where would I sleep if you got another man?" Matthew stated casually, secretly trying to calm his fast beating heart.

Pulling herself together, Beth stepped out of Matthew's embrace and felt a cold rush of air where his strong arms once were. They had hugged many times, but tonight, her hormones made a little tingle in her tummy and lower at the dream of what else he could make warm. Snap out of it she told herself.

"Thank you Hue, but I am just sick of being the only Virgin left in Western Australia! And as much as I love you, I need to find someone who desires me. If there is such a rare species. Come on, let's go. Jo will be waiting and I really want to see her." Beth said by way of trying to distract herself from her saddened love life and raging hormones.

Walking around the car to the passenger seat of Matthews orange Torana, Beth took some deep breaths to calm her racing heart. Please lord don't let me fall for him again she thought. His friendship was way too important to her, to ruin it with her lusty dreams. Matthew got into the car and turned to Beth. Not knowing what to say, he decided for distraction himself and as the engine roared, Jimmy came on the CD player and they "Working Class Manned" themselves to the pizza place. As they sang along together, Matthew reminded himself that he wasn't interested in his best friend like that. She was the most important thing in his whole world and no way was he risking that because his dick stood to attention every time he looked at her. How could he risk a relationship with her when the longest time he had spent with a woman was a very raunchy Australia Day long weekend? He didn't do long term. Screwing up with Beth was not an option. Time to put the acting ability to good use and pretend his feeling for this unbelievable girl were same as same as.

CHAPTER 6

Trying not to glance over at Matthew too many times, Beth was relieved when they finally made it to the restaurant. Being in the confined space of the car made it impossible for Beth not to breath in his clean scent and earthy cologne. He always reminded her of outdoors, and right now, outdoors, away from that intoxication was best for her sanity. Through the glass window, Beth could see Jo sitting at a table in the back. As they made their way in, Matthew held the door for her as she led the way to her new friend. The blush in Jo's cheeks the minute she saw Matthew gave Beth a clue that she also, thought he was nice to the eye. Dam it. He had that effect on people of the female persuasion. And a few same teamers too. Introducing them, Matthew was sweet and very attentive to Jo and the conversation flowed easily.

Sharing the meal as they always did, Matthew knew what Beth would want and took the liberty of ordering for the both of them. Supreme pizza with the lot, no olives. Two Cokes and a small garlic bread. When Jo ordered a small salad and a Diet Coke, Matthew groaned. Another girl who didn't want to be seen eating. As if the world would end if a man saw a woman eat a decent meal? Besides, didn't eating help draw attention to your mouth? Surely girls should… wait. Matthew stopped his train of thought when he realised he was staring at Beth again. Well not all of her, just her soft pink lips. Fighting the urge to see what they felt like on his, Matthew re-focused on the new girl. What was her name again? As Beth moved in the booth next to him, the momentary brush of her thigh against his made his temperature soar. Excusing himself to the bathroom, Matthew, for the second time today needed to reposition his manhood into a less obvious manner. The blonde he took between classes had drained a small urge from him. They had got quickly acquainted in the disabled toilet of the Library. But here the groin salute was again, ready for action. Splashing his face with cold water, the closest thing to a cold shower he could manage, Matthew glared at himself in the mirror. Pull your shit together he cursed at himself.

Jo took a deep breath when Matthew left the table. She couldn't believe how good looking he was.

"Why didn't you tell me your best friend was hot?!" she giggled across to Beth.

Beth felt a chill go through her. Shit. She knew it. The SOB was just too good looking.

"Oh, is he? I guess you could say he is yeah." Beth aimed for cool, calm and collected, but it came out more as rushed, fake and jittery.

"I wish I had paid more attention to my clothes before coming out. He is so mouth-watering I couldn't even bring myself to eat a thing!" Jo exclaimed.

Saved by having to respond, Jo's phone rang cutting the girl talk short. Planning her exit strategy, Beth was grateful to Lori for giving her a reason to leave ASAP. Poor Matthew, I hope he didn't mind having another girl slobbering all over him. If any slobbering was going to be done it should be her…hearing her name snapped Beth back to the present. Something about meeting on Saturday night? A little hard to focus when your brain is mush. Really, the way Matthew was watching her eat should have been enough of a clue that she was not his type. If pizza was there, she was going to eat, and the way he stared at her mouth with that furrow between his eyes made it bloody obvious she had no chance to make him see her as a sexy prospect. Not that she wanted that or anything. Ahhhhhhh!

Ending the conversation, Jo explained that her cousin, waiting forever to call her, invited her to a party on Saturday.

"I will have to check with Lori that we don't have any plans first. But yeah, thanks, a party sounds like fun!" Beth replied as Matthew approached from the loo.

"What is this I hear about a party?" Matthew asked as he slid into the booth next to Beth.

"Jo's cousin invited her on Saturday and she wants to take me as moral support." Beth said turning to Matthew, and wondering why his collar was wet.

"At this stage Beth, I know you more than I even know him. You have to come. I will die without you!" Jo said, a little too enthusiastically for Beth.

"She will be there Jo, this girl loves to dance" Matthew said giving her a squeeze.

"Hue is just jealous of all my awesome moves. Let me check with Lori first ok?" Beth deflected not knowing why this party sounded like a bad idea.

"You should come too Matthew, I mean, if you want to? It should be good." Jo said leaning over the table in an attempt to show more cleavage than was necessary at a dinner table.

"Thanks Jo, if my boss here says I can, I will. Cheers for the invite. Are you sure your cousin won't mind?" Matthew replied playfully, discreetly looking away from the boobage.

"I will just tell him you are my security detail and have to stay with me all night." Jo blushed at her boldness.

"Sounds like a plan, hard work sticking to you all night, I'm not sure how I will manage." Flashing his sly and sexy smile Matthew snuck a look at Beth, noticing her frown.

"Time to go and check on Lori I think" interrupted Beth, rising from her spot.

Matthew took the hint as he smiled over at Jo and moved his way out of the seat. As the girls hugged goodbye, Matthew flashed a wink at Jo as he escorted his best friend out the door. Did Beth seem pissed off? What was that all about Matthew wondered?

Silence was the main topic as they drove back to Beth's apartment. The tension between them seemed to stretch on until Beth let out a curse.

"Shit! I was meant to get Lori some soup. Do you mind swinging around to the Chinese place she likes and you hate?" Beth asked.

"What is wrong with her this time?" Matthew sighed with disbelief.

"What do you mean?" Beth said shocked at Matthew's bitter remark.

"What I mean is, why are you always waiting on her hand and foot? Can't she get her own food? Better still, she could have come with us, saving you the hassle of bringing something home." Matthew fumed.

"Matthew! What has happened to the both of you? I get a strange feeling something is going on. Oh my god you slept together didn't you? STOP the car! I am getting out. I can't believe this. Why didn't you tell me?" Beth blurted as she felt herself rise into hysteria.

"You have got it so wrong Bee. Couldn't be further than the truth actually." Matthew said simply.

Beth's over reaction shot a thrill through Matthew. Was she jealous? Why would it bother her so much if he hooked up with Lori? Pulling into a laundromat carpark, Matthew killed the engine and turned to Beth. Not knowing where he was headed with this, Matthew said,

"Beth, look at me. Yes, I have a problem with the girl, but that is only because of the way she treats you. I don't think she is good enough for you. I swear I have never, and will never make a play for Lori."

Taking a calming minute, Beth asked what she had always wanted to know.

"But why Matthew? Why have you never hooked up with her? She is gorgeous. Irresistible I would say. And you are not a shy boy. I have never understood why you would opt to spend so much time with me. I assumed for a long time it was so you could be around her."

"You aren't so bad yourself you know." Matthew whispered close to her ear.

"Don't be ridiculous Matthew," Beth stated putting more distance between them

"I am what I am, no need to sugar coat it because we are friends. Look, I am worried about her ok? Something is going on and I would never forgive myself if I wasn't there for her when she needed me. She is different to how everyone sees her. She has had a tough life so far and I just want her to know she isn't alone."

"OK. But the Mother Teresa crap has got to stop. You have a lot to offer and maybe it is time someone took care of you for a change." Matthew demanded.

Shit, where did that thought come from. Matthew suddenly felt the urge to be the one to do it too. This was deeper than just being horny. He knew he cared about her, but was it the L word serious? Just keep swimming he told himself as he started the car and headed towards the fast food joint. Waiting in the car, Matthew tried to come to terms with his love for Beth and how much that had changed from the sibling/friend love they had shared for so long. She had no idea how amazing she was. And she never asked for anything in return. But what was this crap about sugar coating? She was bubbly, and full of life and dam if that wasn't sexy as hell. Driving Beth back to her apartment, Matthew was at war with himself. He would be a selfish prick if he screwed this up. Getting out of the car to hug his girl goodbye, as Beth leaned in to kiss him on the cheek, Matthew couldn't control himself and turned to receive her soft lips on his. For too short a time, their lips met with such sweet possibility. It was an electric current running through his body and as Beth gasped and stepped back he wondered what he saw in her twinkling eyes. Did she possibly feel the same? Fumbling back quickly, Beth was adorable in her flustered state and it made him want her more.

That is until she said

"Uhhhh, sorry mate, must be a full moon making me throw myself at any available man. I'll see you later. I want to get this soup to her before it gets cold."

And with that, she was gone. Matthew felt his heart sink. Talk about a slap in the face. Probably what he needed to bring him back into reality. Mate. That's how she saw him. Well fuck, that stung more than he thought it should. Cranking up the AC/DC did nothing to quiet his thoughts as he drove to his childhood home. He was numb. Not able to shake this feeling, a date with a bottle of Beam would be all that soothed him tonight. Maybe things will look different in the morning.

CHAPTER 7

Beth raced for the apartment with her whole body on fire. The softness of his lips and the magical way he tasted would be etched into her brain forever. She almost fainted it was that damn good. It was not as if it was an actual kiss though she reminded herself. Just an accidental brush of their lips. But the reaction she got from it told her she was in danger of wanting more from her best friend than he would ever be willing to give her. She knew his type. Yes she was blonde, but she could not compete with the size 8 girls that usually hung off him. I mean, look at the way he flirted with Jo tonight. This fantasy world of hers was getting out of control and she blamed it all on her lack of experience with the opposite sex. Of course she was into him. He was amazing to look at. But deeper than that Beth knew she had always loved him with a longing to be his one and only. She had been fighting it for a long time. Some distance this week might be a good thing. Would she still see him on Saturday night she wondered? Five days. Beth gave herself five days to get a grip. But they had never not seen each other for that long. Only when she went on holiday with her family and half the time he came too. Focus on study this week she told herself.

When Beth came into the room, Lori was rushing to sit like she had been looking out the window. Showing no indication she saw anything, Lori smiled up at Beth as she brought the dinner to her on the bed.

"You look a bit better than last time I saw you" Beth said, aiming for distraction.

"I really am, thanks. And I will feel a whole lot better after I have this, thank you Beth, you are the best kind of friend."

A little taken aback by the outward display of affection, Beth knew how hard it was for Lori to break down the wall. It was about self-preservation plain and simple. The less she showed to the world, the less there was to be judged, hurt or controlled. Her strength in her adversity, her brilliant brain and her determination was what Beth admired so much. She had moved past the outright idolisation and more into an honest shared friendship, but still, Lori was the confident, stunning young woman Beth wanted to be. Life seemed too far from what she wanted sometimes. So having a best friend so brilliant would have to do.

Allowing Lori to eat her soup, Beth did her night time routine, the pyjamas soft material calling her name. The moment she longed for all day was glorious as she took her bra off and got comfy. Slippered feet padded into the kitchen, setting the kettle to boil and Beth occupied herself with making the drinks, determined not to dwell on the taste of Matthew. Tonight was about investigation. She was going to find out what was going on with her friend. Trying desperately to hold the strings of her friendships together, Beth felt like her happiness bubble was about to burst and the pressure that was building up had her worried. Beth had spent the last fifteen years pinching herself that she could be so lucky to have the friends she did. She never felt like she deserved them. Who was she really? People knew her name simply because she was always with Matthew and Lori. Girls talked to her to get the inside scoop on Mr McHottie, and boys were always nice to her in hopes of impressing Lori. A fact that both of her friends had exploited from time to time. Pulling on her big girl panties metaphorically, as her physical ones were already on, Beth braced herself to get to the bottom of the issues with Lori.

Placing the steaming cup of tea next to her friend, she made herself comfortable on the dark haired girl's bed.

"O.K. Here are the facts as I see them. You have not been well. You have not been happy. And you are working too much. What I want to know is why? So spill it girl." Beth said with meaning.

"Oh no you don't, I want to know what I just saw out that window." Lori replied.

"What do you mean?" Beth tried to say nonchalantly.

"Did you or did you not just kiss Matthew James goodnight?" Lori asked.

"I always kiss him goodbye, as I do you. I'm a touchy-feely person, deal with it. and you are trying to avoid my questions." Beth retorted, hoping to sound calmer than she actually was.

"Hmmm ok, denial time for you, but I will admit, I haven't been feeling too well. I don't know what to tell you Bee." Lori conceded.

"Well let's go through it slowly. What are your symptoms?" Beth probed.

"Vomiting…"

"Wait, really? How much are we talking about here?" Beth questioned.

"Every day for the past five days. But it's not just that that worries me Bee. I don't feel well. I don't feel like studying. Running is sort of keeping me going, but I feel tired and useless." Lori stated.

As Beth contemplated what she knew about the situation, older boyfriend, lethargy, vomiting…Oh boy, hold the phone.

"What happened to that Ethan guy? Have you talked to him about any of this?" Beth hedged.

"I cut him loose a few days ago. He was starting to talk about future plans, even a holiday together. The sex was good but I needed to nip that in the bud quickly before he got too attached." Lori declared.

Ooooookaaaaaay, that explained why Beth hadn't seen him for a while, but didn't stop her worry.

"Lori darling, is there any chance you could be pregnant?"

"Shit Beth. You know I am the smart one here. What do you think? No, I'm not pregnant. But thanks for the vote of confidence in my ability as an adult!"

Startled by the outburst, Beth jumped off the bed and walked around to her side of the room.

"Lori, was there any need for that. I was just asking. Let's face it, all those symptoms are the first things you think of in pregnancy. So sue me for asking."

"Well. I'm not pregnant ok. Can we drop the whole thing? I am sure I will get over whatever it is."

"I don't suppose you will consider going to the doctor to get checked out? I will go with you if you want?" Beth pleaded with hope.

"I will think about it. Give me a few days to go to class and get this semester underway and you can smother me after that alright?" Lori said feeling babied.

"Deal!"

It wasn't the answer Beth was searching for, but it was a step in the right direction. Beth changed her plan of attack with the distraction of popcorn and movies.

It was Lori's turn to pick and as she put 'Never been Kissed', on Beth got the feeling Lori was trying to torture her. She joked the first time they saw it that Beth should have played the lead role. Was this her way of making fun of her again? That icky feeling returned as Beth lamented the complicated life she was living compared to where she thought she should. Too much Drama. Nodding off to sleep somewhere between the carnival and the ball scene, Beth's dreams gave her no peace as she found herself wrapped in the arms of Matthew, doing more than kissing.

CHAPTER 8

Turning the alarm off, Matthew cursed at the thought of any kind of work in his current state. True to his word, his date with the bottle had him blissed out into oblivion last night. But man, he was paying the price now. The five am shift at the Warehouse was hard, dirty labour, and he usually relished the chance to keep in shape. Today was not going to be fun. A five-hour shift with a quick shower and a late class. It seemed like the longest day in all human history. Dragging his sorry arse to the bathroom, the cold shower did little to wake him up. What would the chances be that there was any food in the house? Dressing quickly in his Hi-Vis work gear and steel cap boots, Matthew made his way to the small run-down kitchen.

With a surprise, Matthew noted there was milk in the fridge and a box of cornflakes on the bench. But without a clean bowl, nothing was going to happen. Looking at the large pile of dishes, Matthew tried to count back the last time he was home. Three days. And his guess would be that this was three days' worth of crockery scattered over the peeling benchtop. Rolling up the sleeves of his work shirt, Matthew filled the sink with warm soapy water and made quick work of the mess. Let's face it, no one else was going to do it. Mum was working two jobs, and his lazy arse brother barely left his room. As for Keith, his oh so loving step father, dishes were not in his skill set.

Jesus, his poor mum. How did she end up working so hard to

support the no good bludgers in her life? It was strange to Matthew how he could still feel so protective of a woman who had hardly had anything to do with him since he was four years old. Del and Vince, Beth's mum and dad had been more of a nurturing influence in his life. He couldn't blame his mum though. Being left with two small children, a mortgage, and no close family around, Carol had no choice but to work where and whenever she could. Being left with friends and whoever would take them, as soon as Josh turned eight, they were home on their own. Josh was a good brother until he discovered the magic of weed and the allure of alcohol. By the age of ten, Josh was constantly stoned, drunk and out all night. Matthew was the one who made the lunches, stocked the fridge and did the washing. Not easy when you needed a ladder to reach the washing line.

The first time Matthew went to Beth's house, he was afraid to touch anything. How could a place be so clean? And the smell of those cakes baking instantly made his mouth water. It was like walking into a fairy-tale version of family life. Meals eaten at the dinner table every night, dessert if you ate your vegetables, vegetables full stop. Matthew had learned everything he knew about food from Del Holden. And the thing was, he loved broccoli. Any vegetable Del served him he ate happily, because he had no idea when his next real meal was going to be. And it was just an added bonus that it pissed Beth off when he got dessert for eating his dinner and she didn't. His favourite thing of all at Beth's place, was when her mum made vanilla slices. The smooth custard in the middle and the delicious pink icing was Matthews's all-time favourite thing to eat in the entire world. And Del still made him a tray every birthday and Christmas. That's the kind of woman she is. A mum to everyone, as selfless as her daughter and one of the reasons Matthew was who he was today.

Finally finishing his suds work, Matthew left the rest to dry as he made himself some breakfast and ate it standing up against the sink. The James's didn't own a dining table, probably because they ate dinner in front of the TV every night. That's when they ate together. Which was rarer than a blue moon. His mum had stopped leaving instructions for dinner years ago, when it became increasingly obvious that her second husband was as useless as the first. Keith was a sometimes truckie, hauling loads from Perth to Kalgoorlie. Since being laid off five years ago, he picked up occasional work when he was sober enough to drive. The sweethearts met at the local Belmont pub where mum worked as a bar tender. Every Tuesday and Thursday Keith would come to play darts and have a few cold ones after his two day round trip to Kal. He started coming around on weekends and even attempted to take the boys fishing once or twice. Josh hated every minute of it, but Matthew loved the freedom of the water and the idea of being able to feed yourself. Those memories of good times were very old and very scarce though.

Washing his bowl and heading out to his car, Matthew tried to remember when exactly he started to hate the man that dictated over his mum. So many times Keith let Matthew down, but the final straw for Matthew was the day of his footy final against Kewdale. Matthew had had a ripper season, fairest and best for under 12's and the leading goal kicker three years in a row. Once Matthew started running, no one could catch him he was that fast. It was an away game, so the extra distance to the field left Matthew needing a lift. His mum had made sure there was food for a healthy breakfast before her work cleaning at the shopping centre. There was petrol in the car, and his footy jumper was washed and folded waiting for him. The only thing missing was Keith to drive him. Nowhere to be found. Matthew was stranded. If they had a phone maybe he could call someone. Ten minutes to the game, with a ten minute drive to the ground, Matthew started walking.

As he made good time, Matthew had reached Leach Highway when a car beeped from behind him. Vince Holden, in his old Holden Ute, was the best thing Matthew had seen his whole life. Apart from his feisty daughter that is. Without a word, Mr Holden drove Matthew to the ground and patted him on the back as they got to the ground just before quarter time. It wasn't until after the game, which they won 112 to 64 that Matthew had found out what had happened. Apparently Beth was so worried as to why Matthew was not at the game, she cried uncontrollably until her father had agreed to go and check on him. Her love and thoughtfulness towards him on such an important day was what made him realise what he was missing from his own family. And it was another lesson Matthew learnt about not relying on others for anything you wanted.

The mindless lifting and sifting of his job at the small whole foods warehouse kept Matthew's brain from wandering to other topics he didn't want to face. Vowing to keep a little distance between himself and Beth, Matthew was hurt from her reaction to their kiss. Slightly amusing really when millions of girls were throwing themselves at him, and the one he actually wanted seemed to be horrified with the idea of kissing him. No more dwelling on it, Matthew told himself at morning tea. And while he showered for Uni in the work change rooms, he told himself again not to think about Beth. While driving, he had a stern talking to himself again, as he tried to calculate where Beth would be at that exact time. At least his late class had him pre-occupied with avoiding toilet bang blonde as he had been referring to her.

As Matthew tried again to focus on his note taking, a text came through and his heart raced with the possibility of it being Beth. Too distracted to listen to what his Lecturer was saying, Matthew subtly checked the message and his breath caught in his throat as he read the name on the screen. She had messaged him. This was a good thing right? It at least meant that she had gotten over the kiss and he could just pretend he wasn't in love with her. With a shaking hand, Matthew opened the message and frowned. Beth was at Royal Perth Hospital with Lori. They came in an ambulance and Beth had no way of getting home. Packing up his gear, Matthew did not hesitate to leave the class and go to his girl. It wasn't her fault he was a total sap and had fallen in love with her. Wait, technically it was her fault but shit, nothing was going to stop him from getting to her.

CHAPTER 9

When Beth got home from work she knew instantly something was wrong. Lori's unmade bed, the cup and bowl on the table and the deathly silence in the apartment stopped Beth's heart in worry. With a sudden urgency, Beth searched the home, stopping in her tracks at the sight of Lori lying unconscious on the bathroom floor. Running through her DRABC's Beth was thankful for her first aid training. Breathing was shallow but pulse was strong, Beth got no response from Lori when she tried to rouse her. Calling an ambulance was essential. Cursing herself for not being more forceful with Lori about seeing a doctor, Beth did her best to keep calm as she dialled triple zero.

The ambulance took only ten minutes to reach them and the full siren and lights special made the distance to the hospital seem small. She had been told that she was stable, still unresponsive, with her blood pressure dangerously low. They suspected she had internal bleeding and had prepared the hospital for their arrival and then need for emergency surgery. The whole situation was out of Beth's control. As Lori was wheeled into theatre, a shocked and petrified Beth was left in its wake. Beth reluctantly called Lori's parents, and after several minutes of their questions, Lori's mother conceded that she should come to the hospital.

Not being able to talk any more, Beth simply texted Matthew rather than call. She needed him right now, more than she needed anyone else. She needed to put aside her confusing feelings for her friend and take the comfort he would offer her. Plus she would need a ride home. Sitting in the plastic chairs, in the unforgiving fluorescent lights, Beth felt a pounding in her skull. The pressure feeling was all over her body in fact, the same tight strangle hold on her that had been following her around for months. Now was not a time to cry she told herself as she fought back a sob. As Matthew made his way into the noisy emergency waiting room, her resolve faltered however and when Matthew took her in his arms the dam broke and tears splashed his chest. Beth didn't know how long they stayed in each other's arms, but eventually she found herself sitting once again on the hard seat. Matthew was next to her, arm around her as she rested her head on his shoulder.

He was so warm, so strong and just his presence was holding her together. He was the other half of her, making her feel complete and in that moment, nothing that had happened between them had mattered. This was her safety base. The place she felt most like herself and right now, with Lori in emergency surgery, Beth was not ready to give Matthew up. She would take whatever comfort or love he would offer her. It would be enough. It would have to be. She needed him in her life in whatever form she could have him and if that meant they would only be friends for the rest of their lives, then Beth would learn to deal with it.

Still no word from the doctors and Matthew could feel Beth's tense body close to his. It made him a bastard but he was grateful to Lori for getting sick. This chance to hold Beth in his arms and give her the support she had always shown him was too good to be true. This was all PG stuff though, no lust involved here. This was Matthew, with his heart full of love not lust he realised. The way she cared for everyone. Her compassion and genuine concern for the happiness and wellbeing of others was the most amazing thing he had ever witnessed. This girl, his girl, had fire, strength and love and he wondered if he would ever feel like he deserved her. Seeing Beth cry had destroyed him. He felt like punching someone or tearing down a wall to get answers, but all of that would mean having to let her out of his arms and nothing was going to change that. He was where he was meant to be. She was his home. His love and the best thing in his life by far.

After several hours, Beth was called into the closed ward leaving Matthew alone in the waiting area. Only one visitor was allowed at a time and Beth felt stiff and cold now she had left Matthews arms. He hadn't let go of her once since he arrived. His touch grounding her and stopping the dangerous, sad thoughts that had were now swirling around her head again. Praying to which ever God would listen, Beth begged for Lori to be ok. The guilt Beth would hold knowing she could have helped prevent this would destroy Beth. But thinking the worst was not what Beth did, so she quickly tampered down the negative thoughts and focused on the task at hand. She was going to see Lori and see for herself before panic set in. The nurse explained that Lori was out of surgery and that they had managed to stop the bleeding. As the nurse led Beth to a curtained cubicle, Beth let out a gasp as she saw her best friend laying still on the hospital gurney.

Waking up, Lori had the strange sensation she wasn't where she remembered being. Her apartment wasn't this bright. And that dam beeping noise was not anything she could register as hers. Her groggy eyes swept the area and found Beth staring at her with tears in her eyes. Why was Beth crying and where the hell was she? As Lori tried to sit up, she felt an incredible pain in her stomach and Beth rushed to her side followed by a nurse. Lori couldn't believe it. She was in hospital? "What happened?" she croaked through a dry throat.

"You had surgery Lori. I found you on the bathroom floor and you wouldn't wake up. I don't know how long you were there before I found you. I am so sorry. I should have made you go to the doctor sooner. This never would have happened." Beth cried.

"Hey, enough of the water works ok, I'm obviously alive so we can chalk this up to me being a stubborn bitch ok?" Lori said with difficulty.

Handing Lori a glass of water with a straw as she could not sit up, Beth gave the nurse the third degree. The only reply that came was that the doctor was doing his rounds and would be with her shortly to explain what had happened.

Beth stayed by Lori's bed and held her hand. Now that she saw her friend, her heart eased a little, but they still needed answers. The doctor came shortly after and explained that Lori had stomach ulcers. Several ulcers had burst in her stomach causing her to lose blood internally and pass out. As the doctor explained the dangers and care of the condition Beth found herself feeling down, not relieved. Stress was a major cause of these things the doctor had said. The warning signs were there sure, but Lori's life was great. Beth couldn't understand what Lori had to stress about? Now she was out from under her father's control, life seemed to be getting better for Lori. Not that she had much to worry about anyway. Finishing his instructions, the doctor told Lori she would need to be in hospital for at least another two days, and that Beth should go home as Lori needed to rest after the surgery. She hated leaving her alone, but Beth knew there was nothing she could do for her friend while she was dirty, tired and hungry. Gently hugging Lori and promising to bring her some treats the next day, Beth slipped out of the automatic security doors to a waiting Matthew.

As Beth returned to the waiting room Matthew knew he couldn't leave her alone tonight. She looked wrecked, but somehow, in her saviour costume of messy hair and dark circled eyes, Matthew thought she was the most beautiful girl he had seen. This was his girl. The one that held everyone else up. The fighter that stood behind you when you needed her, and stepped in front of you to take the bullet. She literally took his breath away.

Driving Beth home, Matthew couldn't put his feelings into words. The car ride was a comfortable silence as he held her hand the entire drive. You only need one hand to drive right? Matthew was determined to not let her go until she wanted him to. Unlocking the door with his key, Matthew put the kettle on while Beth got changed in the bathroom. Keeping a few extra clothes at Beth's house, when it was his turn to use the bathroom, Matthew gave himself a stern talking to. Including a harsh word to the little head in his pants - reminding it that tonight was about helping Beth emotionally, and that little Matthew should stay down.

Snuggling up in bed with their cups of tea, Beth flicked channels trying to find something they both liked. Even in her distressed state, she didn't want to upset Matthew. What luck! 'True Lies' was just starting. Action, comedy and Arnold. A classic they both liked. When they had finished their teas, Matthew pulled Beth closer in the bed and cradled her in his arms. His warmth seeped into her bones once again and Beth became very aware of all the points their bodies were touching. Was it just her, or was the temperature rising in the room? If she thought this was bad, her core temp went to boiling in the strip tease scene, as she imagined having the confidence to do such a thing in front of this lovely boy holding her tight. Matthew shifting himself a little, snapped Beth back to reality, and she used it as a chance to distance herself from him a little.

"I think I'm ready for bed Matthew, but if you want to keep watching you can" Beth said, turning onto her side away from the gorgeous boy.

Hopefully, she thought, he wouldn't have noticed her flushed cheeks.

"I will sleep too. Good Night Bethany." Matthew said quietly as he flicked of the TV and slipped down into the covers.

Trying to calm her racing heart, Beth was hyper aware of every move Matthew made, and every muscle in her body ached to turn over and give him a proper good night. Beth laid awake for hours, listening to her beating heart and Matthews's soft breathing. When he started to let out a soft snore, Beth finally felt herself relax and slip into sleep.

CHAPTER 10

Waking the next morning Matthew wondered what the silky softness he could feel was, until he opened his eyes and realised he had his arm around Beth, his hand cupped her left breast as they spooned in their sleep. Shit he thought, even in his subconscious he was a dirty bastard. Slowly and ever so carefully Matthew lifted his hand and moved into a more appropriate position. One that didn't involve impaling Beth with his morning erection. Running through times tables in his head to try and get his body under control, Matthew dared not to look at Beth. He had watched her sleep a number of times, and her long eyelashes and fair hair was messy and natural and the Beth he liked the best.

Beth stirred and turned towards him and like a magnet he went to her, loosely lifting the golden hair away from her eyes to get a better look. Never had he felt like this about anyone. He knew she loved him, but what he felt for her was bigger he was sure. He never saw her get nervous around him, she never looked at him like he was looking at her now. They had never even kissed really, and he could feel his lips tingling with the desire to change that status. Catching himself, he realised he had moved towards her lips and it took all of his energy to stop the forward motion. That brief touch of the lips a few nights ago flashed in his mind, nowhere near enough for him. Next, he saw her quick retreat and that sobered him up.

With a deep shuddering breath, Matthew willed himself away from her personal space, but the movement woke her and those blue, happy eyes smiled at him. That deep breath he first took was a life saver as suddenly all the air left his lungs at the sheer beauty of his best friend. Led by pure desire, Matthew leaned forward and brushed a feather light kiss to her lips. Beth took her own deep breath and as Matthew locked onto the sparkle in her eyes, the same look he remembered seeing before she ran away from him, he couldn't help himself once again. Never loosing eye contact, he tempted fate once again and moved with purpose. The softness of her lips on his, had him moaning in pleasure. And when she kissed him back, his body went hard, in a manner that no amount of reciting times tables was going to fix.

When Beth opened her eyes, she felt as if she was being watched. Seeing Matthew looking at her with his bed hair and stubble, Beth felt the room spin. He was so bloody sexy. The miniscule touch of their lips had her body in shock, and when he came at her again, with those perfect, experienced lips, it took her a few seconds to comprehend what was happening. She was kissing her best friend! And oh man did it feel good. No worry about morning breath, no self-conscious covering up her ample body. Just the press of their lips and the burn in her tummy and lower. But what? Why was this happening? Was he really awake, or was it some sort of dream he was having about one of his Barbies? Wait! Beth thought. Am I the one dreaming? This is too good to be true.

Pulling back, Beth took a calming breath and saw the confusion and terror in Matthews face. So it was a mistake. And now he regrets it big time. Jumping out of bed, Beth raced for the bathroom and locked it behind her, avoiding the disappointing conversation she guessed would come next. I didn't mean to. I thought you were someone else. I am sick of you slobbering all over me. She couldn't hide it any longer could she? He knew. Now he knew and now she would lose him for sure. Splashing cold water on her face, Beth fought back tears. Finally, she had kissed the man of her dreams. Finally she had looked into his eyes and showed him the true nature of how she felt. Finally, she had felt passion and a connection to someone that made her body hum and her heart pound. And it was *finally* she thought. It may well be the final time she saw him.

Matthew sat and willed the door to open. But every passing minute made him realise he had ruined it. What was he thinking? Or what part of his body was he thinking with more accurately? She looked like she was going to cry! Obviously that kiss didn't do the same for her as it did for him. As Beth had fled to the bathroom with the speed of an Olympic sprinter, Matthew felt his heart drop but it was the only thing that was down. Just one kiss had his blood boiling and his body straining to get more of his best friend. Man she was hot. And she definitely knew how to use her mouth. As Matthew wondered who it was that had taught her, he felt a stab of jealousy that it should have been him. All these years, he could have been showing her what real pleasure is. Shaking his head he had to remind himself this this was not what she wanted. This wasn't about what he wanted. This was about not losing his life source over a simple kiss. A sizzling hot, leave you panting kiss, but one that seemed unlikely to happen again. Maybe he wasn't as good a kisser as he thought he was? Could it be that the only person he really wanted, was the first person to resist his moves?

Not able to stand this head maze any longer, Matthew got dressed quickly, shoving the aching stiffness into his jeans and left. As he headed home, Matthew wished he had left a note but what would he have said anyway? Sorry my kissing was so bad it made you cry? Sorry I didn't rock your world but you rocked mine? Really. Just sorry. Matthew cursed himself as he realised he had taken advantage. The moment feeling right to him was just a manifestation of the growing feelings he was having over the year. Beth was in shock. She was vulnerable after the trauma with Lori, exhausted and needed a friend. And what did he do? "Fuck!" he shouted, not caring who heard him.

That kiss would have to be in his spank bank and locked away. Something he would never forget, but never get again. She deserved better than him he reminded himself. Someone who doesn't maul her when she simply needs comfort. But so help them, Matthew would be on their arse if they hurt her. The thought of her with anyone else made him nauseous. Space. He needed some space. Sitting at the lights, Matthew sent Beth a quick text saying he would see her on the weekend. Three days would be coming up to the longest they had been away from each other in a while. It will give him time to straighten himself out and work out what to do next.

Beth replied quickly with a reminder of the party for that new girl and her cousin. Right, something to keep him occupied. He just needed to work out what to say to her. He was torn between admitting he wanted to kiss her again and stepping back so she could find someone worthy. What good would it do him though he thought? Twice she had run away from him. The first time had been a mere touching of the lips. The second, a full, sensual taking of what he wanted. He wasn't stupid enough to put himself through that again. Not unless she would stick around. Third times a charm? I guess we will see soon enough. But right now, he needed to focus and get his mind off Beth. Nothing like a few shitty days with his family to distract him.

When Beth heard the door close her tears came full force. No holding them back. OK so she didn't have that much kissing experience but surely the look of terror on his face was a slight overreaction? I can't be that bad! From her point of view it was the most amazing thing she had ever felt. Maybe he was trying to make her feel better, but when he realised how gross she was, he regretted it? Beth was glad he was still coming to the party. It meant that she hadn't lost him forever. She would see him on the weekend, and apologise for making him uncomfortable.

Now to put him out of her mind. God knew she had enough other things to keep her busy. Emailing her lecturers, and then Lori's, Beth explained the emergency hospital trip and the reason for her absence. Next, Beth texted Jo and asked her to take notes for her. First week and she was going to be behind already. That flutter of anxiety flickered through Beth and left her struggling for breath in the middle of the bedroom. Her eyes wandering to the empty space Lori would normally be filling, and then to her own bed, the scene of the crime. Back and forth her eyes moved in desperation, searching for answers that weren't there. Beth squeezed her eyes closed and pulled herself together.

Beth left for the hospital shortly after, calling in to pick up some flowers, some skittles and twenty Carmelo Koalas. She had after all, promised her friend a treat. Following her path from the previous night, Beth was shocked to not find her friend where she left her. The rise of panic setting in, Beth sucked in some calming breaths and approached the nurse at the desk. Not being family, Beth was refused information and for the second time in the day she let the tears flow, unable to stop the cyclone of feelings controlling her.

Apparently sitting in the middle of a hospital floor, sobbing, raises some concerns, and Beth was quickly shown to a quiet room to have her breakdown. At first Beth thought they were escorting her to the Psych Ward. At this point, let's face it, she might need it. But no, she was in a tiny meeting lounge, with comforting pictures of landscapes and an urn to make tea or coffee. When the nurse returned, he made Beth a cup of tea, and subtly checked on her stability. Finally calm, again, and warmed by the sweetest cup of tea she had ever had, Beth laid her head on the table and counted her breaths. Paul, a middle aged nurse, with scruffy hair and a kind face interrupted her at breath 312. They were letting her see Lori.

CHAPTER 11

Stepping into the hospital room, Beth was taken aback by the pale colour of her friend, and the amount of tubes still attached. Her guilt set in a thousand fold as she pushed her own worries of lust and hot kisses aside. This was the world in perspective. Lori needed her and was going to be Beth's only mission right now. Placing the flowers on the window sill of the private room, it was obvious to Beth that Lori's parents were footing the bill. Only the best for their daughter it seemed. Even though they didn't approve of her choices behind closed doors, in the view of the public they would exude care and parental responsibility. Strange, because actually caring for their daughter and taking an interest in her life would be a hell of a lot cheaper.

Lori laid resting amongst a nest of pillows. Investigating the new room, Beth quietly pulled a soft looking chair close to the bed and took a long look at her friend. She looked younger. Yes, she was pale, and thin, but the creases were gone from in between her eyes and her mouth was soft and restful, out of its usual thin lipped scorn. Shit, Beth thought. What has been going on?

With nothing else to do, Beth fired up her laptop and checked the emails to see if her messages had gone through. Satisfied with her own account, Beth logged on to Lori's again, and had to squint closer to make sure she was seeing accurately. One hundred and sixty unread emails. Normally very efficient, Lori hated having unread mail, and was always super diligent in checking and discarding. The oldest one Beth could see was from two months ago.

Aiming to be helpful, but feeling like she was bordering on stalker, Beth started deleting spam and other junk mail. As she did, new items came in, obviously waiting for the full mail box to be cleared. After an hour of clearing and sorting, it seemed Lori had only 32 important messages, which Beth began to read with curiosity. Countless emails from lecturers, asking for due work, and unexplained absences. Library accounts for overdue books, and a worrying email from the Dean, concerning her failing grades and her enrolment at the Uni.

Nearly dropping the laptop in shock, Beth looked once again at her friend laying in the sterile hospital bed. The shattered pedestal Beth had held her on filled Beth's eyes with tears anew, but she was determined to hold it together this time. This wasn't about how sad she felt about her hero worship, this was about Lori and her problems. Slipping from the room, Beth made her way down the hall until she discovered another secret breakdown room like the one she was escorted to earlier. Getting to work, Beth contacted all of Lori's lecturers, informing them of her current status and formally applying for a break in her studies until further notice. No way was Beth letting Lori lose her dream without a fight. But she was going to want some answers when that girl was well again.

It was getting close to lunch time when Beth returned to the hospital room, and much to Beth's delight, Lori was sitting up, awake and watching television. Beth noticed with a smirk that several chocolate wrappers were strewn around her friend.

"Hello sunshine!" Beth managed cheerfully despite her insides churning with worry.

"Oh, you're here. Hi, I thought you had just left these on your way to class."

"No such luck darling, you are stuck with me all day! I am glad you knew they were from me. I did promise you a treat did I not?"

"Yeah, thanks. Not sure what the nurses will say, but chocolate IS a cure for everything right?"

Beth smiled, "You know it. Do you want anything else?"

Taking a while to answer, Lori sighed. "No, I'm...I just need to rest. You might as well go you know. I won't be very good company."

"So what is different about that? You are always terrible company! Everyone knows I am the fabulous one in this relationship! So, sorry, but you are stuck with me! I will let you rest when you need to though, but friends stick together, and you my darling, are my best friend."

"Really? Hasn't pretty boy got that claim on you?" Lori couldn't help herself with the dig at Matthew.

Beth felt her heart flutter at the sound of his name, but was determined to ignore those feelings. Now was not the time to unload on her friend and ask for advice. Which sucked really, because Lori was the only one Beth felt she could ask.

"I am here with you. You are my priority, and you know very well how I feel about you. So stop trying to get rid of me and deal with the fact that your roommate is still your roommate where ever you go. Look at the time. I am going to pop to the caf to get myself some lunch. You want anything?"

"If I say I want a coke, will you quit asking and fussing over me?" Lori gave in.

"Sure thing, and find us something good to watch during lunch will ya? There is bound to be some pathetic reality drama or talk show we can laugh at." Beth said as she stepped out of the room. OK, so the situation was bad, Beth thought on the short trip to the unappealing cafeteria. If Lori was using her 'don't smother me' attitude, it usually means she is suffering and trying to be tough. Getting the truth out of her was going to be tricky. Using some reverse psychology might be needed. But how to out psych the psych student?

Getting back into the room, Beth sorted their treats and got comfortable as the watched "Pawn Stars". When the food was finished, Beth laid back in the chair and risked a glance at Lori.

"I know I said I would stay, but it's obvious you don't won't me here, so, I will leave you alone ok?"

"It's not that I don't want you here, it's just, I don't know how to explain, and I know you are dying to ask me loads of questions." Lori said barely looking away from the TV.

Smiling inwardly at her skills with working her best friend, Beth replied "Hey, no questions, just concerns. I want to make life better for you so this doesn't happen again ok? So talk, or don't talk, I will only stay if you want me to. This is all about you, so you are in charge ok? I know you like that!"

With a deep sigh, Lori turned to her friend and tried to begin. Where to start? Really, what was wrong? And how could Bethany, always happy girl possibly understand the dark emotions inside Lori?

"It's been going on for months. The stress I mean. I have been thinking about it a lot, and the trigger point was when 'He who can't be named' broke up with me. I know it is stupid ok? I know it makes no sense. I mean, it wasn't just that. It's the school stuff too, but what he said to me, what he did…I guess it was the final crack to the egg."

As Beth sat silently listening, Lori could see her forcibly holding back questions, and she appreciated that from her friend. Beth really was the only human who saw all of her and accepted that as good enough. Were her parents in the hospital annoying her? No. Not that that was what she wanted, but still, it was obvious there was no one else coming. So this was what friendship really meant then.

Yes, Lori knew very well she had control over the girl in front of her, but there was more to the relationship now, than Lori could ever have imagined. At first, it was good to have a puppy who paddled after you and made you look good in front of others. But it had changed from hero worship to real friendship over the years, and now more like a sisterhood.

Lori thought guiltily about how superior she had always felt. But as Lori reflected, was that really her attitude, or was that her parents influence. Hell, they always think they are better than everyone else. And they expected the same from Lori. But being away from them, on her own, with Beth, Lori suddenly felt lost. As if she had no personality or thought of her own. She was now questioning who she was, what *she* believed in and when the realisation came that she was blank, her world started to crumble.

"You know, I can see you are bursting over there, go on, I will give you one question, so make it a good one."

Beth contemplated her next sentence. So much she wanted to ask. Was he really worth it? Have you seen your parents? What has happened to your grades? The question she went for was a little self-serving.

"Why have you never told me any of this?"

"Honestly? I don't know Beth. I guess I have been in denial so long I never thought there *was* a problem. And doing these psych units has made me realise I need to be the patient not the therapist. Everything I thought was important and good about myself is fake. I used to think I could do anything, that I could contradict my parents and be successful on my own terms. But now they will know they were right. Why didn't I tell you? Because I couldn't even tell myself how low I had fallen. You are so happy all the time Beth. You make the most of every situation. Nothing ever seems to bother you. How could you possibly understand how much pressure I felt under?"

"WHAT!" Beth shouted. And then remembering where she was, she dialled down the drama. "How can you say that I am always happy? I have spent most of the last twenty four hours a blubbering mess worried about you, and completely confused about Matthew, and I have spent my whole life in your shadow wanting to be just like you!"

"What a waste of time."

"No." Beth said as she lowered herself gently on the side of the hospital bed.

"There have been times I have hated myself because I am so different from you Lori. You laugh, and have fun, and people are drawn to you. You can have any boyfriend you want. You have such beauty it literally blinds me some times. Hello, Virgin sitting over here! I am far from happy Lori, but I am hopeful and I think that's what you have lost."

"What a mess we are hey?" Lori sobbed as she felt months, maybe years of tears raining down on her.

Beth wrapped her arms around her friend as they sobbed together for what felt like hours. Taking a steadying breath, Beth drew back and made sure Lori was looking right into her eyes.

"We will fix this Lori. We will work together and get your hope back ok? I need you Lori. And I know that sounds selfish of me but it's true. My whole life I have felt lucky to have you as a friend. I am not letting a trip to the hospital and this little pity party of yours change anything!"

Not capable of talking yet, Lori simply nodded her head as her sobs continued. It was a needed release but drained her until she had no feeling left at all. Waking up alone in the dark, Lori checked the clock. 2am. SHIT. Beth must have left her without Lori even knowing. As thoughts flooded her mind, Lori was left with the biggest red flag of all. What did Beth mean when she said confusion about Matthew?

CHAPTER 12

2 am. 2 am and Matthew was wide awake and going crazy. It had been another hopeless night with his brother and his Stepdad, resulting in Matthew having retreated to his room and having finished all of his readings. Hell, he even started an assignment that was due in six weeks. Yep, he was desperate. A whole twenty four hours without seeing Beth, and this was meant to go on for two more days? Just as Matthew was about to give up the pretence of sleep and play Mario cart, he got a text.

Curious as to who it would be, and hopeful it was the one person keeping him awake, Matthew turned on the side lamp and found his phone. Nope, just the opposite in fact. Evil incarnate. But with a sudden flash of concern, Matthew opened the message knowing the one thing he and Lori had in common was Beth. One sentence.

"Man up or leave her the fuck alone."

Right. OK. There was only one 'her' that she could be referring to. Beth. And he was well and truly used to Lori telling him to fuck off. But wasn't she in hospital? Why send a message like this at 'why the fuck are you awake o'clock'? Does this mean Beth has talked to her about the kiss? He was never going to sleep now. The idea of those two talking about it somehow made it seem dirty. Not gossip to be aired in a hospital room. But girls did that stuff didn't they? Talked to their best friends about the boys they liked? Or in this case, don't like. This was not good.

Matthew was sure Lori would be advising Beth to stay away from him. God only knew that Lori wasn't Matthew's biggest fan. Beth had never listened in the past, but maybe now, after he threw himself at her? But what was with the 'man up' shit? Matthew could only dream that it was Lori giving him a go ahead. It did sound like an ultimatum. One *or* the other. Matthew was beginning to realise that there was no way to 'leave her the fuck alone.' At this point, it was all or nothing, and Matthew was ready to put it all on the line.

Knowing Lori would not be expecting a response, Matthew turned his phone and light off, letting his mind dwell on all the possibilities. Finally, Matthew started drifting off to visions of Beth, dancing with him at the party, their bodies close, her arms around him. It seemed like a premonition not a dream, and it helped him with a plan of action as he floated into peaceful sleep. His last thought before everything faded was needing to just get through the next two days until he could make it work.

Beth woke up with a start. Where was she? Having silently retreated from the hospital room, Beth had made it only half way home before she had succumbed to exhaustion. Finding herself at the BP carpark, Beth checked her phone for the time. 2 Am. Groaning while she stretched, Beth surveyed the petrol station carpark. Dead. The station was still open, but it didn't look like too many people needed fuel this time of night.

Thankful for the lack of audience, Beth unlocked her door, and made her way in to use the facilities. After a loo break and a quick face rinse and brush of the hair, Beth realised she was not going to get anymore sleep. Scanning the shelves for something reasonably edible for breakfast, Beth settled on a mini serve of Nutrigrain and a Masters Chocmilk. Paying the cashier, who looked barely old enough to dress himself, Beth returned to her car and sat in the florescent lighting of the BP sign to eat her makeshift meal.

There was something peaceful about being on your own out in the world this time of night. Fresh air, even with the slight petrol tang, clear skies, and silence that seeps into your bones. Tomorrow, Beth would be back at the hospital, and focussing all her energy on getting Lori better. How, she had no idea. Cracking open her laptop, Beth started searching key words like 'stress' and 'breakdown'. Making notes, Beth started to feel confident she could help her friend get back to her best.

Not realising how long she had been researching, Beth was struck by the beauty of the sunrise. Like a re-birth of her emotions, she felt ready and able to tackle the day. Heading home for a shower and resources, Beth felt her own hope rising and preyed it would rub off on Lori. With no time to think about Matthew, Beth moved through the apartment with purpose and was soon on her way back to the hospital, even singing along with the radio.

Armed with photos, craft supplies and determination, Beth found Lori sitting in a chair by the hospital window. Cup of tea in hand, and dark circles under eyes. At least she had some colour in her cheeks Beth thought. Looking up at Beth, Lori let out a groan when she saw the supplies in Beth's arms.

"Death by scrapbook? You really are trying to kill me Beth" Lori commented from her perch by the window. She made no effort to move. She was tired yes, but not from her own mental cyclone. She felt a sense of purpose for the first time in a long time.

"We are going to make vision boards" Beth said choosing to ignore her sarcastic friend. "Well, a vision board and a friendship board I guess. I really want to get us both from our past, to looking at what we want for our future. If you build it, they will come!" Beth said in a mocking voice making reference to an old Kevin Costner movie her mum loved to watch. Unrolling the cardboard sheets and laying them on the bed, Beth smiled inwardly as she noticed Lori hadn't protested too much.

So for the majority of the day, breaking only for food and eventually a nap, Beth and Lori talked, cut, stuck and glittered like they used to a decade ago. The friendship board, filled with photos of them together at various stages, they worked on together, each making notes and adding sparkle. In the centre, was a black and white photo of Beth, Lori and Matthew taken at Christmas when they were ten. It had always been one of Beth's favourites, because instead of the three of them side by side like usual, they had made an 'F' with their bodies. 'F' for friends. All three had huge smiles and even Lori commented on what a fantastic day that had been. After the reminiscing, Beth marched Lori forward like a drill Sargeant, going from past to future dreams. People who plan for the future, are more likely to see it to fruition, or so Beth believed anyway.

Beth was relentless but Lori was not going to argue. This girl always made Lori smile with her positiveness. It literally shone out of her and Lori was happy to bathe in its glow for the day. Besides, it's not like she had anything else to do, anywhere to go. But what did she want for the future? This was the confronting part. A psych degree would be great and all, but Lori would have a lot of her own issues to confront before she could go too much further with that. She was eighteen! Surely by now she should know what she wanted out of life?

Lori always had a plan. It was always set by her parents though. This time, faced with what she really wanted, and what she really needed, she came up blank. Beth's question tugged Lori out of her internal wanderings and Lori had to get her to repeat the question as the fog cleared from her mental journey.

"You do know you can change and change again right? You have a brain picture there, which from my Freud 101 for dummies, suggests that is your psych class. But what else do you want to do?"

Seeing the look of concern on Lori's face, Beth quickly added "It's not meant to be a stressful question, I am so sorry. We can just forget it if you like?"

Lori smiled and turned to look at her friend properly. Did she realise how much she was helping? Probably not. And Lori had certainly never admitted her worth. Lifting her chin, Lori replied;

"Writing. Literature. I read enough books. I think I would like to learn how to write."

Lori watched her friend's face for signs of disapproval. That's what she would have seen in her parents' faces. But Lori should have known better. Her friend, with the sunshine glow, beamed at her as she pulled her in for a bone crushing hug.

"That is the best idea ever. You would be great. And psych knowledge with a literature degree would be so useful. Maybe you can teach the rest of us how to survive by writing a book!"

"I can't change my course now though. My parents would never pay for something else." Lori said wistfully.

"It's called a vision board because it states what we want for the future. None of this has to happen right now. This is long term ideas babe, and I expect your first dedication to be to me, for making you do this vision board in the first place ok?" Beth stated with a laugh.

Suddenly feeling a little lighter in the head and the heart, Lori started making notes on her board. Unlocking her own dreams and wishes and letting her imagination run wild, Lori felt an enormous surge of freedom and hope. Christ, if this kept up she would be humming show tunes and skipping along the halls like Little Miss Sunshine over there. That thought didn't make her cringe as much as she thought it would either. This girl has done so much for her, Lori was determined to not let anything or anyone dim her girls light. It wasn't on her vision board, but Lori knew that in her future, she would be doing everything she could to take care of her quirky, silly, spontaneous and colourful friend.

CHAPTER 13

"What's got you so jumpy?" Joshua growled as Matthew recovered his senses at the kitchen table. He had fallen asleep with his head resting on his books and his brother's midnight snack had woken him abruptly. He looked up through foggy eyes and lines on his face from the fold of his book.

"Dreaming of being out of this place." Matthew replied as he tried to remember his crazy dream. Of course there was only one thing he dreamed about these days, and at this point, his dreams were the only thing keeping him sane.

"Shouldn't you be reading that shit not drooling on it?" Josh smirked as he slapped jam on a piece of bread and left the fridge door hanging open.

Matthew sighed, got up and put the lid back on the jam, placed it on the shelf and shut the fridge. Too tired and confused to deal with his brother at this ungodly hour, Matthew started collecting his books when Joshua shocked him with an almost tender moment.

"I'm worried about you Hue, you seem even more of a loser than normal, what's going on? Where is your nun?"

Freezing at the insulting nickname Josh used for Beth, Matthew had a big decision to make. Drop his stuff and sock his brother in the jaw like he had wanted to do for years, or walk away. Why did he have to be the grown up?! Glaring at his useless brother, he began moving out of the kitchen, still fuming but too weary to start this shit now. One day soon he was going to have to deal with that dickhead, but right now, he had to get some sleep.

"Hmmm, maybe not a Nun then hey little bro? Has she finally walked on the wild side with you? Not your usual type though hey? Bit more on the chunky side, but hey, I guess something to hold onto is always…"

Josh didn't get a chance to finish the sentence. Matthew had him pinned up against the fridge in a split second. His books scattered on the floor where he dropped them.

"I suggest you keep your mouth shut now, or I will have no problem with making you sip through a straw for the rest of your life." Matthew hissed in his brothers' ear.

Joshua, now over the shock of the ballsy move, pushed his brother off him with a smirk.

"Well aren't we the little knight in shining armour? Good to see you still have some life in ya Matty boy. Was starting to think you had turned all boring stiff on me."

"Can't you just leave me the fuck alone Josh? Seriously, you have never cared what I do, never been a role model or even a friend, so just stop pretending you know anything about me OK? And leave Bethany out of it."

"No you little shit, you listen to me. We all get that you hate it here, you want to make better of yourself. Fuck, I wanted that once too. But you might as well face reality little Bro, you won't make anything of yourself moping after that chick. Little miss hoity toity and her stuck up friend are nowhere in your league. If you are going to bust your balls for something, make it worth it."

As Matthew turned to walk away, he couldn't argue with his brother. He had similar thoughts himself. He wasn't good enough for Beth. But what Josh didn't understand was that it was Beth that gave him the strength to better himself. Yes he did it to feel worthy of her, but he also did it because she believed in him. She seemed to be the only one who ever had. What had happened to his brother to make him so cynical? God knows home has never been the font of positivity, but this seemed deeper than that.

"What happened to you Josh? Why are you this bitter, cynical old man already when you are only in your twenties? OK I get that you have lost hope in the big bad world but why shit on me man?"

"You get told you're no good I guess you start to believe it at some point." Joshua mumbled and then tried to cover with a cough. An awkward silence stretched between them as they stared at each other from across the small run down kitchen.

"Anyway, not everyone can be the golden boy can they?" Joshua threw out sarcastically breaking the silence in the room. "No way to disappoint people if they don't expect anything from you in the first place right? That's why you a have your knickers in a knot little bro. You're mum's last hope. No one gives a fuck what I do and they never have. You though, oh boy does the sun shine out your ass or what?"

"You're jealous of me?" Matthew couldn't believe his ears. "You used to be so strong. I wanted be just like you. I used to think that I was lucky because at least I had a brother that was cool, and strong and who believed in me. And what do I get? Your pissy arse pity party. Poor Josh, no one loves him. No one cares what he does so he can be the biggest dick of all time. But guess what? I loved you. I believed in you. I needed you. And what I get is a shell of a brother who spends all his time feeling sorry for himself instead of making his own life better. Fuck anyone else man. Fuck what they say. Have some fucking pride and find that person you used to be and prove them all wrong. And don't shit on me for trying to do that because if you care for me at all, if you know me at all, you'd know the best thing you could do for me, is be the brother I need you to be." Practically shouting at this point, Matthew drew a deep breath and turned his back.

With tears in his eyes and a raw throat from his emotional exorcism, Matthew trudged to his room. Exhausted from his outburst and desperate to escape, Matthew threw himself on his bed and prayed for sleep. He faintly heard footsteps outside his room as he finally drifted off. It felt good to say what you mean and mean what you say he vaguely thought as he faded into a dreamless, deep sleep.

Listening outside the door, Joshua hesitated. Half wanting to walk in and give Matthew a slap, the other half of Josh acknowledged what was said as the truth. He had given up. He wasn't who he once was. But what Matthew didn't know was the reason for the breaking point six years earlier. That was a secret Joshua was determined not share. He could never let Matthew know the truth.

"So let him hate me." Joshua thought as he moved quietly back to his own dingy room.

Trying to push the stinging words aside, Joshua laid on the bed staring at the ceiling. This wasn't a life. This was a cycle of despair. Not easy to get out of when it has been all you have known for six years. The kid was spot on. He was stuck in his own pity party. Bad things happen all the time. Kids die of cancer, starving refugees, some seriously bad shit happens all the time. What right did he have to sulk? But he had never talked about his problems so maybe it was poisoning him from the inside. And Damn, if he wasn't a little jealous of Matthew. He had been through the same shit and yet he kept going. Maybe that Nun was worth the hassle after all. Josh sat wondering where the fuck he could get himself a bit of Nun. One thing was for sure, he was going to lay off the little shit for a while.

Lighting up a fag, Josh paced his dilapidated bedroom. Rank smelling, dark and littered, it had become his cave. Like a shell protecting him from the reality of his life. Josh always assumed his life sucked because his mum forced his real dad to leave. He always blamed her. But flashing back to that night six years ago, when he tracked his dad down, his whole life had shattered. Rather than the heartfelt reunion he was looking for, he was hit with a hard knock of shitty reality. His father, having remarried, sat with his happy family, arm around his son, and barely acknowledged Josh when he approached. Ushering Josh to a side door, the father that Josh had always wanted, warned him to never come near him again. So, he was happy now. He had a son and a daughter. And his new wife knew nothing of his first family. Carol hadn't kicked him out. He had left.

The realisation of not being wanted had taken all humanity and hope from Josh. He had built this man up in his mind, because he honestly thought his mum was to blame. Now, faced with the facts, Josh had stayed locked in a vacuum of despair. Tonight though, he felt a crack in that shell. An awakening of sorts. Butting out on an overfilled ashtray, Josh once again flopped down on his bed. Squeezing his eyes shut, Josh took a mental punching bag to his thoughts. Stop the shit. Time to move on. But where to start? Fucking no way in hell he was asking his little brother for help. He seriously doubted he would get an answer anyway. He could always ask the Nun. Shit. Bethany, call her Bethany if you want her to help you idiot. Ok. Plan of sorts. Daylight, and he would contact that girl. Wait, what day was it? Saturday already? No matter. She seemed to be a miracle worker. Time to see if she could work her magic on him.

CHAPTER 14

Stretching out of the cramped visitors chair in Lori's room, Beth had lost track of the days. And boy was she glad about that. Her mind had one single focus. And it had seemed successful to some degree. Too early to tell, Beth knew, because this sort of thing was going to take time. Checking her phone, with a start, Beth realised it was Saturday all ready. How long since he had seen Matthew? Hopefully her hormones had died down a little by now. Not that it mattered. She wasn't going to that party now anyway. Would he still go? Beth wondered. It would be a good thing if he did she reminded herself. Jo could do with a friendly face. O.K. Time to get busy thinking about something else before the green flush of jealousy returned.

Making use of the private room facilities, Beth freshened up and returned to a wide-awake Lori. Every day, colour was returning to her friends' cheeks, and that sparkle was shining in her eyes again.

"Good Morning Sunshine!" Beth exclaimed when she entered the room.

"Hey there energizer bunny" Lori replied playfully. "So, what's on the agenda for today? Finger painting? Matching tattoos? Some other form of BBF torture?"

Laughing fully, Beth skipped her way over to her friend and hugged her. It was tough to express how she was feeling when she had to be gentle with her friends' fragile body. She really felt a bear hug was in order.

"Today is rubbish movies and popcorn day" Beth stepped back and looked at her friend. "And also, getting you cleaned up day because, oh boy do you stink!"

Enjoying the breeze of life that was her friend, Lori could feel herself smiling. Actually smiling. Not the fake, yeah, I'm ok smile she had used so often. An honest to god, full lips and teeth smile. And so it began. True to her word, Beth, with the help of a nice female nurse, got Lori in the shower. Beth washed Lori's hair as she sat on the shower chair in protest. Combing out the long dark lengths, and blow drying it was relaxing and bonding.

Half way through the movie "Ever After" another Drew Barrymore classic, Beth's phone beeped with a message. Sneaking a peek, Beth cringed as she forgot to cancel the nights plans with Jo. Firing off a quick text, letting the new girl down gently, Beth decided it was a good time for a break. Taking the long path to the cafeteria, Beth felt a little disappointed about not going out. But she knew it was for the best. Lori had seemed so much like herself again today. Her old self, not her Uni self, and Beth felt a little proud. The line was a long one, but Beth was OK with that. Things were getting back on track for her best girl, and that meant Beth herself felt a million times lighter.

Feeling relaxed and at peace, Lori sighed a deep and thoughtful sigh. How different she felt at this moment. Such a contrast to five days ago. Disturbed by another beeping of her friends' phone, Lori picked it up and punched in the code. No secrets between these girls. 2384 – BETH on the keypad and Lori looked at the latest message. Frowning, Lori re-read the new message and then scrolled to see what her friend had sent. Hmmm, not good she thought. No way was Beth spending another night in these boring four walls when she could be at a party. But how was Lori going to get her to leave? Pressing the call button on her bed, Lori had an idea that could possibly work. Now to get more people on board.

Not long after the nurse had left and agreed to Lori's plan, Beth's phone rang. Without hesitating, Lori answered it with her usual greeting "Yeah, speak…"

Totally shocked and unprepared for such an abrupt reception, Josh had trouble consoling this harsh voice to the ever-bright goody two shoes that hung around his brother. "Ahhhh, who the hell is this?"

"Excuse me, you rang this number buddy, who the hell are you?" Lori spat back at the rude imbecile on the other end.

"This is Josh, Matthews' brother. Is that Bethany?" Josh spluttered in complete shock.

"Oh shit, no. This is Lori. Beth's not here. What do you want? All ok with lover boy?" Lori suddenly felt bad. If anything had happened to Matthew, Beth would be devastated.

"Ahh, no, Matthew is OK, I just needed…I just needed Beth's help. I ahhh, didn't have anyone to ask. I know she goes all mission helper sometimes and well, fuck, I don't know, I just thought she could maybe, come see me? Listen, it's a stupid idea ok? Don't mention it. I ahh, I will…I will work something out."

Feeling kind of bad for the guy, Lori knew this was the kind of thing Beth would normally throw herself into. Maybe what Beth said about helping others helps herself was worth a shot? "Listen Josh, you remember me right? I'm actually in the hospital right now, and Beth has just headed out to eat. I can give you my number. I'm not as saintly as Beth, but I'm stuck here for at least one more day, and well, you have a captive audience since I can't leave. Why don't you come down and see me?"

Josh was kind of frozen in disbelief. Was this the same ice princess? At this point, who was he to judge though? And shit, she was in the hospital? What kind of bastard would he be if he said no to someone sick that was willing to hear him out?

"OK, ummm. Can I come and see you tomorrow? Like, what kind of things do you want? You want lollies? They always make me feel better. You want like flowers or some shit, I can bring you…"

"Josh, calm the fuck down dude" Lori interrupted his rambling. "I don't want anything, it's cool. Just come when ever, Beth has me covered for snacks. It's not a date you idiot, just come and see me and we will talk. In fact, I think you can probably help me a little too."

Lori hung up the phone and smiled. Huh, maybe the douche had a few brain cells left and might be useful to Lori's plan for Beth. Or more accurately, her plan for Beth and Matthew. Cos' no matter how much she disapproved of the boy, it was clear Beth was head over heels for him. And it was pretty obvious the boy was into Beth too. Had been for years. Both of them seemed oblivious to how each other felt though. What they needed was a little push in the right direction. And if Josh made himself useful, maybe it could happen in this lifetime.

Rushing to send a text to Matthew via Beth's phone, Lori hit send, just as Beth re-entered the room with an arm full of sandwiches and drinks. Discretely hitting the call button, Lori signalled the nurse in the pre-arranged manner. As Beth sat down in her usual chair next to the bed and unloaded the bounty, Lori couldn't hide her smile. Time to give the girl back some of the love she gave out to others. That boy better deliver, Lori thought as she acted like nothing had changed.

CHAPTER 15

Beth was enjoying the chill time as she watched the rest of the movie with Lori. At least her friend still had a smile on her face. Munching on the left-over lettuce from her sandwich, Beth was surprised when the nurse and the doctor both came in looking serious. With her stomach in knots, Beth stood up and took Lori's hand.

"It has come to our attention Miss Holden, that you have been spending time outside of visiting hours in this hospital." The doctor said sternly. "I am sorry, but there have been complaints and we are going to have to ask you to leave and come back during visiting hours tomorrow. If not, I will have to have you removed, and that would mean you might not be invited back."

Beth gasped. "I...I... I... what? What do you mean there have been complaints? I have done nothing wrong. You hardly even know I'm here!"

"Please understand, it is nothing personal Miss. It is simply hospital policy. You wouldn't want these lovely nurses to get in trouble would you?" The Doctor said smoothly.

Knowing that was the killer blow, Lori fought to hide her grin. "Oh shit, so sorry Doc. Beth really didn't mean to upset anyone. She is all I have. But we understand. We don't want to cause any trouble. Please, she will go now and return tomorrow. Just give us a chance to say goodbye ok? Thank you, thanks for being so understanding."

The doctor and nurse both smiled as they left the room and Lori knew she had to thank them later for their Oscar performances. "Hey Beth, don't worry, I'm fine. Seriously, I'm pretty tired, I will just sleep this afternoon. Haven't you got things to do anyway? Wasn't there some sort of party?"

"There is no way I am going to a party while you are in the hospital Lori. What kind of friend would that make me?" Beth said in a rush. She was distraught and annoyed and pissed off and anything else she could think off.

"You would be the kind of friend that goes out and has a life so she doesn't end up the same as me, that's what you would be. I thought you said this Jo girl needed you? I can't be that selfish and keep you to myself, now can I? Besides, I am planning on you coming back to spring me out tomorrow. Go, dance a little, and have fun. And I expect a selfie or too as proof you went out ok? You must be dying to see stalker boy by now?" Lori threw that last comment in as a tease. But the reaction she got was strange.

"Yeah, I guess, I haven't seen him for a few days. And Jo was disappointed." Beth replied solemnly.

Sensing Beth wasn't ready to talk about it, Lori eased off on the teasing. "Well, give me a hug then girl, before they call security on you."

Wrapping her arms around her friend, Lori hoped with every fibre of her being, that Beth made it to that party. Matthew was going to be there. Lori had made sure of that. With a final light squeeze, Beth finally left and Lori laid back on the bed and closed her eyes. Only time will tell if her plan had worked.

As Beth stepped out of the hospital, she felt somewhat lost. The sudden jolt back into dealing with her own life left her in a daze. Go to the party? See Matthew? Well she guessed nothing could be worse, so why the hell not. Heading home for a soak and a nap, Beth drove home in relative quiet and came to terms with what was going to happen. Sick of all the drama and heavy feelings, Beth decided to be open to the night and just enjoy herself.

Taking a relaxing time, glad to be home, Beth washed and dried her own hair, for the first time in days. Applying a small amount of makeup and her favourite pink lipstick, Beth felt good as she made her way to the party. Texting Jo to meet her out the front, the girls hugged a greeting and made their way inside. The mysterious cousin, Corey, greeted Beth with a friendly hug and a long perusal of her chest. Not that Beth was complaining. Blonde, crew cut hair, bright blue eyes and a confident smile, Corey was cute.

When he asked her to dance, Beth thought it would be rude to say no, so she slipped her hand into his, as he led her to the temporary dance floor for the evening. As if the guy had planned it, a slow dance came on, and Corey gathered Beth in his beefy arms and swung her around. Giggling and enjoying the sensation of being held, Beth relaxed and felt herself move with the music and the adorable guy holding her. Three songs later and Beth tore herself away from Corey, feeling guilty for bailing on Jo.

As she entered the kitchen on her search for her friend, she came across Matthew, leaning on the door frame. Feeling her heart stop, Beth forced herself forward casually, reached up on tip toes and kissed him on the cheek as she went past, "Hi Hue", and she continued forward.

Reaching out, Matthew grabbed hold of her arm and spun her back to him. Cheeky, he thought, but damn did it make him feel good. "That is the greeting I get? I haven't seen you for days, and you spend hours out there on the dance floor with Fabio over there, and all I get is 'Hi Hue'? I protest. I demand more."

Giggling like a school girl, Beth wrapped her arms around Matthew and squeezed. She wasn't sure how seeing him was going to go, but this was better than she thought. Almost as if the kiss never happened. Wait, is that good thing or a bad thing? "OK, is that better? I actually came looking for Jo, but I guess you will have to do!" Beth said with a smile on her face.

"Huh, I'll take what I can get. How about we show these stiffs how to really dance?" Matthew said quietly in Beth's ear as he led her over to the makeshift dancefloor. Never letting go of her hand, Matthew pulled Beth close and began the moves they had practiced so often. They moved seamlessly together and Matthew felt like he was flying, spinning Beth, and dipping her low all the while she giggled and glowed against him. They were a team, and Matthew was glad the oops I kissed you incident was behind them. Even though he wasn't entirely sure he wanted it behind him. Scooping in to whisper in her ear, Matthew felt a tap on his shoulder.

Fabio was standing there, puffing his chest out and Matthew felt the urge to laugh. Beth quickly covered his reaction with an introduction. "Matthew, this is Corey, Joanne's cousin, Corey, this is my best friend Matthew." Beth explained.

"Well, hello there Matthew. That's a relief, I thought I had some competition for my girl Beth here. Best friend huh? Guess you don't mind if I cut in then?" Corey said a tad too loudly.

"Actually..." Matthew started but Beth cut him off, "That would be lovely Corey, thank you." She replied glancing at Matthew with a pleading expression.

"Right, OK, no worries, see you around Carry." Matthew said as he stalked off.

As Corey took Beth in his arms, Beth noticed Matthew reach for another Beam and Coke and skull the thing. Trying as she might, her focus could not go back to the man holding onto her waist. Another glance over to Matthew and finally Jo was found, but what Beth saw was not comforting. Matthew was leading Jo onto the dance floor and the smile on the girls' face spoke volumes. Jo was thrilled. Beth, not so much.

As the night went on it was pretty obvious to Beth that Matthew intended to make Jo feel very, very welcome. With his hands and his mouth. Not that she should be noticing, she had her own stud grinding up against her. It was good, it was. It just wasn't as thrilling as dancing with her friend had been. Corey hadn't kissed her yet, but she could tell he wanted to. He kept staring at her mouth when they danced close and his roaming hands were mapping the curves of her ass as if he worked for Main Roads. Beth kept reminding herself to relax and enjoy it.

Ready to call it a night about 2am, Beth searched for Matthew.

Unable to see him amongst the drunk crowd she fired off a text. five minutes later, Matthew replied with a short, 'see ya at the game tomorrow?' Grinding her teeth, Beth gave a two letter 'OK', and headed towards her car. Almost at her car, Beth squealed in shock as she was grabbed from behind. Corey, with his large arms and styled hair swept Beth up and kissed her long and hard. As first kisses go, it had a lot of unwelcomed tongue and overwhelming strength. Gasping for air, Beth pulled away from Corey and noticed his sexy smirk. Maybe operation 'Beth gets laid' is already in action!

"Goodnight beautiful" Corey breathed into Beth's ear and stepped away. "I will call you next week so we can hook up again babe. You, have blown my mind."

Beth lifted her hand in a weak wave. Unbelievable night that's for sure. Time for bed and maybe things will seem a little more real in the morning.

CHAPTER 16

"Fuuuucccccckkkkkkkk!" Beth felt like she had a hangover, despite only having one drink all night. What was this pounding in her head? Dragging herself into the shower, Beth replayed the nights' events over and over in her head. Highlights? If she was honest, the dance with Matthew had made her heart warm and her lady parts tingle. But the interest he showed in Jo clearly signalled his friend only feelings for Beth. She hadn't exactly been a Nun either, so who was she to judge his actions. Telling herself this was going to be a good way to keep their friendship on track, Beth escaped the cleansing spray and dried herself quickly. No need for makeup today. A scratch match to kick start training season for footy. Beth dressed in her club shirt and trackies. She pulled her hair up in a soft pony tail and slapped on a hat. It wasn't a beauty contest today.

Arriving at the ground an hour before kick-off, Beth assumed some of her boys would need some strapping. Making her way into the change rooms, Beth set up her bag of tricks. Five short minutes later, her first customer arrived and the next 40 minutes saw Beth flat out taping shoulders, knees and ankles. Beth loved the comradery in the room, and how they all treated her like one of the boys. A short ten minutes before the game was due to start, Matthew James strolled in looking worse for wear.

"Need me to strap your ankle Matthew?" Beth called out as he changed behind the door.

"Nah, all good, no time" came the muffled reply.

Beth frowned. About to disagree, Beth stopped herself from nagging him. He was a big boy, he could make up his own mind. Walking out onto the ground together, Matthew pointed out Jo and Corey on the sidelines waving. "Seems like we both have a fan club today." Matthew smirked. "Have a good time last night Bethy?" he shouted as he ran off backwards, still watching her as he joined the team.

What the? Beth took another glance over on the sidelines. She couldn't decide what was freaking her out the most. The fact that Jo was here watching the game, in her totally inappropriate high heeled boots and thin leggings, or that she had her cousin standing next to her, waving and smiling. Lifting a hand in recognition, Beth jogged to the bench to gather the water bottles. As the coach greeted her, Beth ignored the questions going around her head and focused on the game.

As it was the first run for the team for the year, Beth was kept on her toes delivering water and instructions from the coach. By quarter time they were down by two points and Matthew appeared to be limping. He had kicked three goals already, despite the fact that he looked a little green under the gills. Getting out the ice, Beth told Matthew to sit on the ground so she could apply the cold pack. Eliciting a few cat calls from the guys, Beth ignored the shouts of "Favouritism" as she did her job. Matthews shouts back to his team mates had Beth shocked into silence.

"Boys, Beth's off the market. Her boyfriend Fabio is over there."

Ignoring the replies of "Don't break my heart baby" and "I will fight him" Beth growled at Matthew. "Who said he was my boyfriend Matthew? I only met him last night!"

"Sorry Bethy, you looked pretty close last night. I just assumed you were serious. Did big stud not seal the deal last night then? Idiot. I would never let someone like you get away if I had the chance. I mean, you were clearly the most beautiful girl in the room. I'm not sure I want you spending time with someone so stupid Baby girl."

Still staring into her eyes, Matthew couldn't believe what had just came out of his mouth. He meant every word, but right now, sitting on a footy field was probably not the best time. Realising that they were getting stares from the rest of the team, Matthew jumped up and handed Beth the ice pack. Turning back to check on his girl, Matthew noticed the flush in her cheeks under the Belmont Bombers cap, and thought how truly beautiful the girl was. Giving her a wink, Matthew sprinted off towards the mid-field ready for the second term.

Meanwhile, Beth wondered where all the oxygen went. And that wink of his. Infuriatingly sexy. Fanning her heated body with the ice pack in her hands, Beth ran back to the bench and tried to calm herself down. Ouch that boy was hot. But what the hell was all this about? Last night he was all over Jo. Maybe he was just overly horny and taking it out on Beth? Either way, that boy was making her smile AND squirm in her seat.

At half time, the team was up by three goals, and Matthew was top scoring with six. Pulling Beth out of the change rooms with him, and with his sweaty arm draped over her shoulder, Matthew made a path way to Jo and Corey. Greeted with hugs all round, and a brief shake of stiff hands, Matthew was relieved Jo didn't throw herself at him again. She was nice enough, but he wasn't really interested. She was a little too high maintenance for his liking. I mean, who comes to the footy in high heels and tits pushed up?

"Wow Beth, you look different without your makeup on and everything. Still pretty, but yeah, different. I didn't know you were such a big part of the team. Lucky I am so good looking, or I might be jealous about all these boys you hang around." Corey said confidently smirking at Matthew.

Muscles going tight next to her, Beth could tell Matthew was not a happy camper. Rushing to intervene, Beth playfully smacked Corey on the arm saying "Ha, no competition at all Corey. I umm, I don't normally dress up for the footy. Too much running around in the rain and dirt."

"That's how we like our Beth, Corey, down and dirty." Matthew said dryly leaving Beth choking back a laugh.

Jo, realising she was being left out of the conversation, stepped up to Matthew and whispered something in his ear. With a look of shock Matthew stepped away from Jo and tugged on Beth's arm. "Don't forget you are needed to strap up some thighs baby girl."

"Umm, bye then. Guess we will see you after the game? Sorry, duty calls." Beth shouted as her friend pulled her away. Curious as to what had Matthew retreating, Beth questioned him. "OK, spill. What did Jo say to you that had running away?"

"Do you really want to know Bethy? Because I am not sure you could handle that kind of talk." Matthew teased, still holding her hand and swinging it between them as they raced towards the rooms.

"Yeah, you're right. I don't think I want to know." Beth replied as Matthew chuckled.

Letting go of her hand, Matthew flashed that easy grin of his and disappeared into the toilets. Beth kept walking to her prep area, finding three patients waiting to be re-strapped. Getting to work, Beth lost herself in the chatter of the team, the smells, good and bad of the blokes, and the strategy talk going on. Walking out with the team, Beth laughed when Max grabbed her from behind and pretended to cry that she was no longer his. Then he kissed her cheek and told her he was happy for her before heading to the back line, ready to knock some heads together. He was brutal, but he had a soft middle and Beth thought of all the team fondly. She fit in here. And she was relaxed and respected.

Running out to give Matthew a drink after he kicked his eighth goal, Beth got a playful pat on the backside and that dangerous wink again. Half way back to the bench, Beth heard the crowd yell, and she turned to see what had happened. Matthew was down, and the opposition full back was getting a talking to by the umpire. What the hell? Beth thought. This was meant to be a friendly. Dropping her drinks, Beth raced to the injured Matthew and tried to assess the damage.

Shit. His ankle. The one she wanted to strap up for him. After a quick assessment, during which Matthew refused to make eye contact, Beth signalled for the stretcher. This elicited protests from her friend. This was not going to be fun. He was not going to be happy when she made it clear he was going to the hospital. The cringe when he coughed made Beth wonder if he had a cracked rib as well. Seeing red, Beth leaped up and got all up in the bone crushers face.

"What the hell is your problem dickhead? It's meant to be a friendly. Can't handle someone kicking your ass hey? You gutless piece of shit, I want to..." with a hand cupped over her mouth, and strong arms pulling her away, Beth didn't get to finish her tirade. The coach dragged her away to the safety of the sidelines before removing the hand from her mouth.

"Whoa there sweetheart, don't get yourself banned, I need you too much. Beth, listen, go take care of our boy ok? And let me know how bad it is." Coach steered her towards the change rooms, making sure she was going in the right direction. As she left, Beth heard the coach say to Max, "Make sure that son of a bitch knows your name by the end of the game ok Maxy boy. He needs an attitude adjustment."

Beth smiled as she pictured her big boy Max making good use of his foot up someone's ass. Reaching the rooms, Beth prepared herself for a battle. This was not going to be fun. And she was right. Matthew refused to go to the hospital. It wasn't until Beth threatened to call *her* mum, that the boy relented. She made fast time to the hospital, and arranged for one of the team to take Matthews car home. Something to worry about another day.

While waiting at the lights, Beth sent Lori a message apologising for not being there yet. Relieved, but curious, Beth wondered how Lori got home after the reply she received. One out of hospital, one in she mused to herself. What a week it had been. X-rays and consults five hours later confirmed a fractured ankle in three places and two cracked ribs. eight weeks' recovery at least. Leaving the hospital late Sunday with Matthew having used every expletive in his vocabulary, Beth swung by Maccas. Even with the Happy Meal, Matthew was not a happy boy.

CHAPTER 17

Using Beth for physical support, Matthew groaned in pain as they made it into his room. Beth had been unbelievable. She never left his side the whole time at the hospital and the way she faced up to the asshole that took him out! He could have kissed her. She was such a fireball when she needed to be. Making it to the bed, the pain to his pride was almost as bad as his fucking ribs.

Moving around the room clearing a path to make life easier for Matthew, Beth felt a wave of exhaustion hit her. Sitting down on the bed next to Matthew, she took off her shoes and wiggled her sore toes. Laying down next to him, Beth was careful not to jiggle the bed. Looking over at her friend, Beth sniffed and moved farther away from Matthew. "You stink Hue!" she said, getting up from the bed. "You need a shower darling."

Half asleep already, Matthew moaned. "And how do you expect me to get in there?"

Frowning, Beth acknowledged the difficulties in that situation. Moving down the hall, Beth located a bucket and flannel. Filling it up with warm soapy water, she returned to Matthew's bedroom on a mission. No way was he staying stinky. Slipping off his remaining boot and sock, Beth was trying to decide the best way to attack when Matthew spoke up, "Bethy darling, is this your way of getting me naked? I am so into that plan."

Feeling a little hot under the collar already, Beth decided to take on this task as she would any clinical operation. They normally would start with the less dirty places right? Start from the top before needing to make the trip south. Placing the flannel into the warm water, Beth leaned over Matthew, and began carefully washing his face. It was like a slow-motion event. She could feel every stroke of his face under the thin material. Behind his ears, rinse, back to that way too dangerous face and strong chin. As she gently covered his lips and moved down to his neck a smile appeared on that devilish face. "You know this is one of my fantasies right Beth? I think you were dressed a little more skimpily though..." Matthew said seductively.

Taking a deep breath, Bethany chose to ignore Matthews taunts and continued wiping over his neck. Gently pulling his head forward, she wiped behind his neck and was startled by how close their faces suddenly were. Still with that infuriating smile, Matthew's green eyes sparkled and Beth was very tempted to close the distance between them. Placing a hand on his chest to steady herself, Beth shook herself out of the thought as she remembered his damaged ribs. "Shit, sorry, your ribs, let me see them." Beth rushed, delicately trying to remove his t-shirt in a way that didn't hurt him.

"You know, anyone would think you only liked me for my body." Matthew joked, then winced as the pain from his chest picked up again.

Helping to remove the footy jumper and bring it over his head, Matthew was in heaven. As Beth took her time with him, her touch and her closeness calmed his sore muscles. It didn't help a certain muscle though, and Matthew prayed Beth was sensible enough to not look too far south of his waist. With her perfectly round chest just centimetres away from his face, he knew it was not deliberate, and he was far from complaining.

Taking that warm cloth and rinsing it again, Matthew braced himself for the contact to his skin. He wasn't in much pain. How could he be, when the girl of his dreams was touching him like this. Imagining it was for a far better reason than to clean him, Matthew closed his eyes briefly but returned to watch those lovely hands work over his bare skin. She was so soft, so gentle and her hands on him felt right. Like everything he needed and wanted in this smallest of touches. As Beth wiped over his chest and moved down his body, Matthew knew she noticed the obvious bulge in his pants. Her cheeks taking a pink tinge, they locked eyes and Matthew felt his heart stop, his breath falter and time stand still. It was like the planets had aligned and he could finally tell her.

And then Beth's phone rang.

Breaking the spell, and shocking them both back into current time and dimension. "Hello?" Beth answered as if she had run a marathon. "Oh, hi Jo. Yeah, um, we are here, why?"

Matthew didn't like the sound of this conversation. Let's face it, he was already uptight over the interruption. His good mood and erection both went down with the next sentence he heard.

"Oh, wow, ok, I will let you in then." Beth said as she made her way towards Matthew's bedroom door.

"Beth wait!" Matthew said a little too loud and a little too forcefully making him wince in pain and humiliation at the same time. As Beth turned back to him she looked flustered.

"Matthew, your girlfriend is here to look after you apparently, so I am going to let her in." Beth said quietly.

"My girlfriend? Since when do I have a girlfriend? And why is Jo assuming she is it?" Matthew said disgusted.

"Well it appears after your close bonding last night, she has appointed herself your girlfriend, so lucky you stud. I will go get her, and she can finish cleaning you up. Though I'm not too sure why she has waited all this time to finally do something, I have been with you all day." Beth stated as she left the room as quickly as she could.

Letting Jo in and guiding her towards Matthews' room, Beth convinced herself that this was a good thing. She could now go and focus on Lori. She was desperate to know who picked her up and honestly, the tension in the air of that bedroom had left her hallucinating. She almost thought Matthew was turned on by her touching him. The tell-tale signs in his pants indicated that. Time to step away for sure.

Saying her goodbyes, she went to leave the gushing Jo to tend to the patient, but Matthew called her back. "Don't I get a kiss good bye Bethy?" he teased. Taking a deep breath, she moved quickly to the bed, bent down to kiss his cheek and as she did Matthew whispered into her ear.

"Thank you for the bath Nurse".

Giving Joanne a quick hug, Beth left with tingles down her spine. He has got to stop teasing me like that she thought as she started her engine. It took the 40-minute drive to return her heated blood to normal. Time for her to focus on Lori. Parking in her usual spot, Beth noticed a familiar looking car. But it was out of context so she couldn't quite place it for certain.

Reaching the door, Beth had a WTF? moment as she walked in.

CHAPTER 18

Joshua shifted in the seat at the table. The look on Bethany's face made him want to run out the door. What was her problem? This was not a good idea, Joshua thought to himself as Beth shut the door, still staring at him. Fuck, it was enough to make a guy sniff his armpits and make sure he had his shirt tucked in. Standing up to leave, Joshua looked over at Lori but as he went to step away, Lori grabbed his arm and spoke, breaking the silence in the room.

"Hi there, you going to come join us or just stand there staring all day?" Lori said as she pushed Josh back down in the seat.

"I, um, I don't know, I'm still trying to work out what dimension I've landed in. Hi Josh, not that I'm not glad to see you but what the hell are you doing her. I mean here?" Beth blurted.

Seeing the blood drain from Lori's face, Beth tried harder to show a poker face. Looking somewhat drained of blood himself, Joshua swallowed hard and spoke up. "I rang yesterday to talk to you, but Lori answered. I ahhh, I came to visit her today at the hospital and she said she needed a lift home"

"Right, of course, because I was att the hospital with your brother…"

"What? What happened?" Joshua questioned rising again from the chair.

"Oh, you know, taken out by an asswipe at footy. He's home now.

His girlfriend is playing nurse, so I wouldn't be too concerned. I am sure she will keep him happy." Beth said with a bit too much venom.

"Shit. Girlfriend? Since when does Matthew have girlfriends?" Lori asked, seemingly back to functional speech.

"Ha, yeah, well it was news to him too, but you know my new friend? After the party on Saturday, she seems to have attached herself to him. I left them to it. Never mind that I was the one with him all day at the hospital. Anyway, not my problem. I am really grateful to you Josh. I don't know what I would have done without you actually." Beth said, defeated and sinking into a chair.

"Now, you rang? Can I help? I'm sorry I wasn't able to help, but it sounds like you and Lori have become friends?" Beth questioned them as she looked between the unlikely pair.

"Yeah, um, I was having a bit of trouble, and I, yeah, I know you are good at that kind of thing. My brother is always going on about it, so I rang. And Lori said she was in the hospital and wanted a visitor so. Yeah, I'll stop talking now." Josh said backing up towards the door. "I'll get going. Thanks Lori, I, yeah, I'll call sometime. See ya later."

As Joshua James let himself out of the apartment, Beth turned to Lori with raised eyebrows. "Right, now, want to fill me in what is going on?"

"I'll put the kettle on. You go have a shower and then we will talk O.K?" Lori said, turning her back to her friend.

"NO! I'm meant to be taking care of you remember? You just got out of the hospital!" Beth exclaimed.

"Beth, I'm fine. And you look like you are liable to fall down from exhaustion. You can't be Florence Nightingale to everyone without taking some care of yourself. Go! Making you a cup of tea is not going to cause me to expire after a week of doing nothing. NO! Don't interrupt. Off you go. And don't come back here until you are clean and relaxed in your PJ's."

Feeling dismissed, Beth did as she was told and made her way to the bathroom via bedroom for nightwear. But the shower was far from relaxing. She had avoided thinking of what Matthew and Jo would be up to right now. But the way Matthew had whispered in Beth's ear, and the affect she knew she had on him was scorched into her mind as she rinsed her hair out. He flirted all the time. It was in his nature. But this, this felt different. Charged. And Beth was nowhere near settled as the shower was done.

Trekking back to start a discussion with Lori, Beth fought the desires she knew were going to plague her. She was in too deep. And she needed a distraction from this drama. Her body was wound so tight. The tension in her muscles and the tingling in her groin was almost unbearable. He was NOT helping her situation all. The time away from him hadn't helped either, as now she felt even more in love with him. Sighing, Beth braced herself for the intense battle she was going to wage with herself. Again. She had fallen for him again and the last time nearly broke her.

When Beth entered the kitchen and sat the table, Lori could tell she was upset. But knowing her friend would ignore her own feelings and want to smother Lori, she decided to play it cool and pretend she didn't notice the loud sigh Beth exhaled as she entered the room. "Don't shoot me, but I made Popcorn too. Yes, it meant two extra minutes standing and waiting for the microwave, but I promise I was multitasking while the kettle was on, so don't freak out!" Lori said poking her tongue out.

Both at the table now, Beth went to reply but Lori cut her off. "So, about Josh. He rang yesterday while you were out getting food. I kind of thought you had enough to do and I admit, I was curious, so, I decided to handle it. The guy wants some advice. Now I know I'm not the best person to advise since my own life is kind of in the shithouse, but he really just needed someone to be honest with him. And that I can do. So, don't worry ok? I think it will be good for both of us actually. Gives me something else to think about other than my own miserable life."

Remaining quiet, Beth took a handful of popcorn and couldn't hold back a smile. This was the first time her wonderful friend had done something like this. Something for someone else other than Beth. Was it wrong to feel proud of her? It's not that she was unkind at all, just she never liked people to see the kindness in her. What a day. Beth was so confused, tired and emotional, she couldn't find anything to say.

Lori took Beth's silence as disapproval, but then Beth smiled and Lori relaxed a little. It wasn't often that Beth was quiet. Things must be serious. Changing topics, Lori was desperate to know something. "So, this Jo girl thinks she is Lover boy's girlfriend hey? Does she realise you want him yourself?" Lori said looking right at Beth. Her reaction gave away the truth. Bullseye Lori thought. But she knew her friend would want to deny it.

"Lori, you know Matthew and I are just friends. Why do you always do this? He doesn't see me that way, and it's none of my business who he goes out with. WE.ARE.JUST. FRIENDS."

"But you want it to be more, don't you?" Lori interjected. "I don't see why you can't just tell him. I think you would be surprised. If you want my opinion, Matthew is just in love with you as you are with him."

Gasping, Beth turned away from her friend. She was certain Lori was wrong about how Matthew felt. But was it that obvious about her own feelings. "Please don't tell him." Beth whispered.

Lori, looking sad, moved away from the table to get into the eyesight that avoided her. "Why? Why won't you tell him? You are going to torture yourself watching him bang your new friend."

"Please Lori, you can't tell him. I got over him once I can do it again. I don't want to lose him as a friend."

"Beth, why on earth do you think you will lose him?"

"Come on Lori, can we just leave it? It's been a big day. How can I possibly explain to you the laws of attraction? I am not his type. You have seen the girls he goes out with. None of them have a waist bigger than an 8, or an IQ higher than their shoe size. If I told him how I felt. If he knew how much I want him, he would be disgusted. And I love him, I do. In every way. But losing his friendship would ruin me more than not having his love will. I need to just move on. Who knows, maybe Corey will be THE ONE? He says he wants to take me out, and frankly, I could do with the distraction right now."

"Corey? Who the fuck is Corey?" Lori ranted. "And he could be THE ONE? Really, when I haven't even met the dude and you have been in love with Matthew your whole life? I get the whole, wanting to be BFF's forever, I do, cos I don't know what I would do without you Beth. But you honestly think he doesn't want you? You have never noticed the way he looks at you? It's sickening really. I've always been jealous of how he worships you. Never once have I been anything to him. He has only ever seen you. I would probably go as far to say as he is the only boy I have never had drool over me."

"I can't do this anymore Lori, I really can't. I need to put him out of my mind. I appreciate your confidence, I do, and I love you for it. I just don't believe he would go for a ninety-kilo girl he has had as a friend for years, over slim, blonde party girls he could have on endless supply." As Beth made her way to the bedroom, she kissed her friend on the cheek and sighed again. Time to put this day behind her.

Watching her friend leave the room, Lori knew Beth saw her bodyweight as an obstacle. Hell, Lori herself had thought it for years. But hearing Beth say it. Hearing how little she thought of herself because of her weight? That was messed up. And Lori was pretty sure Matthew was into Beth. He didn't deserve her, but he wasn't that shallow surely? He wouldn't have hung around all this time without feeling something, would he? Retrieving her phone, Lori sent a quick text.

Cleaning up the kitchen, Lori dropped the dishes as soon as her phoned beeped in a message. Just as she thought. Maybe her partner in crime would come in handy. Taking her pain meds and making her way to bed, Lori was confident in her way forward and she actually felt good. She hadn't seen her parents. Even though she knew they footed the private hospital room bill. She hadn't looked at the full inbox of emails and due dates from Uni. She hadn't even contemplated what washing she needed to do or bills she needed to pay. But she still found herself with a buzzing energy.

Knowing nothing more could be achieved today, Lori made her way to bed, checking on Beth on her way past. She appeared to be out for the count, but the dried tears on her cheeks made it obvious she had cried herself to sleep. Letting out her own sigh, Lori changed her clothes quickly and got into bed. Tomorrow was a new day. She was more than glad to be out of that hospital and in her own bed. Time to move forward.

CHAPTER 19

When Joshua got home, he noticed there were no cars out the front he didn't recognise. Stopping in to check on his brother was a new habit for him, but it sounded like the kid had been hit pretty hard. Knocking on the door, another foreign concept to him, Josh pushed the door open to find Matthew lying in bed reading a book. Did that kid ever stop? He was like the poster child for motivation or some shit. At least he was alone. Mind you, Josh wouldn't have minded checking out this so-called girlfriend. She must have balls to try and settle that player down. Balls, or no brains at all.

Stepping into the room, Josh mumbled a hello and stood at the foot of the bed. "You look like shit little brother. Been picking on the big boys again?" Josh threw at Matthew.

"Something like that. Eight weeks off the field they tried to tell me. Eight fucking weeks. Bet I can make it back in six. Five if I try real hard." Matthew answered, trying to convince himself at the same time.

"I heard you have a girlfriend now Matty boy. How did you let that happen? Not to worry, she will come to her senses soon I am sure. Make sure you keep her around to play nurse for a while though, cos I don't think your girl nun is very happy with you right now."

That got Matthew's attention. "What, what do you mean? Did you see Beth? Did she tell you I have a girlfriend? I don't by the way, but I want to know how you think I do? And why is Beth not happy with me? Fuck Josh, if you are messing with me I will be so fucking mad."

"Relax bro. Yes, I saw her. Yes, she told me you were playing patient and nurse with your girlfriend, her words, not mine. And yes, she wasn't in the best mood I have seen her in," Josh said, knowing he had sunk the hook into his little brother. "I don't know why you care though, that Beth girl has never given out, so you have to fish around I guess."

"It's not like that with Beth, we are just friends. You know this. You said yourself she is out of my league. But I don't understand why she is mad at me" Matthew said gazing around the room. It was like he could still feel her near him. Still smell her and feel her soft hands on him. Despite the unwelcome visitor that had her running away.

"Let me ask you this then ok true? You love her, don't you? You actually love Bethany hey?" Josh pressured his brother. Time to make him fess up.

"What do you want me to say? You know the answer to that or you wouldn't have asked. I love her. I probably always have. But this heart to heart we are having right now? It means shit. For all the reasons you have laid out to me before. She deserves better. She needs better. And yes, I have nearly fucked up the friendship a few times because I can't keep my dick down. But I can't lose her. She's the only fucking good thing in my life man."

"I may choose to be offended by that little bro," Joshua joked, "but do you really think you could lose her after all these years? I mean, you are no picnic to be around. If she was going to drop kick you she probably would have already. You worried you aren't good enough for her or that she will say no?"

"Both" Matthew admitted.

Chuckling and shocked at the honesty, Josh pressed ahead "Well for the record, she looked pretty pissed off when she was talking about your so-called girlfriend. In fact, I would go as far as to say she sounded jealous. You'd be in there Matty, if you wanted to be."

"Why is it you make everything sound dirty?" Matthew mumbled, lost in his thoughts.

"It's a gift! Now you need to step up your game if you want to keep this girl. At least show her what she is missing."

"Why do you even care? This is the most we have spoken in five years." Matthew threw back at Josh as he headed for the door.

"I don't really. It's just sad watching you mope around and when you are with her it means you aren't here. So it's a win for me." Joshua bit back.

"Ha, thanks, so sentimental of you. Now come back here and help me to the bathroom to take a piss, will you? Pretend we actually give a shit about each other because I'm not due for more pain medication for another hour and it hurts like a mother." Matthew pleaded with Joshua.

With a smirk, Joshua helped his brother down the hall and back before he retreated to his own room. Sending a quick text to Lori, he had confirmed both their suspicions. For smart people Beth and Matthew were acting pretty dumb. He could understand Matthew's POV. Not exactly hard to imagine you weren't good enough, but what was Beth's hang up? She could have him anytime she wanted him. Lori seemed like she knew what she was doing anyway. Let her deal with the how and the why. All this touchy feely was giving Josh a headache.

Firing off one last text before he lights outted, Joshua felt a smile on his lips. First time in a while he felt useful actually. And Lori was a firecracker. She had told him about her own fucked up parental situation. He never would have guessed that under that Ice Princess was a real person. We all wear masks after all. No, that wasn't right he thought to himself. His brother was never like that. He was straight up take it or leave it. That's why this drama with his girl didn't make no sense.

Waking in the morning, Josh did the righty and checked on Matthew. Helping him to the loo, they hardly spoke. But as Matthew was lowering himself gently back into bed, Josh had to ask. "So, this girl that thinks she's your girlfriend? What happened to her last night? Couldn't get it up for her so she ran away?"

"Are you always this disgusting? If you must know, her name is Jo, and she's a friend of Beth's actually. She um, I ahhh, I just pretended to get sleepy. She left about twenty minutes after." Matthew admitted.

"Are you kidding me? What a tosser! Just tell her to get out and get it over with! What a wimp."

Matthew cringed at the critique. He was a loser and he did need to cut the girl loose. "I know. I will. Bit hard to be on my game right now. And I, I guess I needed a distraction."

"Understandable. So, what you doing all day?" Josh asked and was surprised at himself for really wanting to know.

"Can't do much with these ribs. I'm stuck for a while. So, reading and feeling sorry for myself."

"Right, good luck with that. I'll be around so give us a shout if you need me to hold ya hand again." Joshua said as he left the room.

As Matthew tried to get comfortable he imagined what Beth would be doing right now. Monday morning her favourite/least favourite lecture. At least she would be able to go to classes. He should probably do something about that. Like email them or something. Just as the thought entered his brain, a text came through. Stretching causing him considerable pain, Matthew grabbed his phone and slumped back on the bed. Beth. Shit. He had it bad. The anticipation of just a friggin text message from her was enough to make him tingle.

Unbelievable. How did she do that? She had been to see his lecturers already. He never asked her to. She just knew it had to be done and took care of it. Took care of him. His reply took him ten minutes to write. He kept deleting and re-writing. In the end he settled on "What would I do without you? Love M xx". That didn't give away too much, did it? Just the usual banter.

Putting the phone down, Matthew closed his eyes and daydreamed of the day before. They had a moment, he was sure of it. Just before her phone rang. She had that look. That she knew he wanted her and she might want him too. There WAS something between them. He could feel the tension. But he knew something was holding her back as much as it was holding him back. Would he see her today? It wasn't in her nature to leave anyone she knew stranded. Opening his eyes, he needed to stop this or itw as going to drive him crazy.

Flipping the book open he distracted himself with human anatomy. It was going to be a long few weeks.

CHAPTER 20

Beth was on a mission. The tears from last night washed away, there was work to do. On campus early, Beth visited all of Matthew's lecturers and explained the medical situation. She gave them all her own email address and asked for them to contact her if anything was needed urgently. They didn't ask who she was, or why she was doing it, for which she was very grateful. Somehow, telling them she was his best friend didn't make her all that happy.

Sending Matthew a text, Beth was ready to face the day and she met Jo as they walked into the lecture theatre together. "Don't ask, don't ask, don't ask" Beth repeated to herself. In the end, she didn't have to ask. "When I left Matthew last night he was exhausted. Thank you so much for taking care of him until I got there." Jo said turning to Beth.

"You know Jo, he is my best friend. I should really thank you for taking care of him so I could go home. I had been with him all day at the hospital after all." Beth said with a hint of sarcasm.

"Oh, well, yes, you're welcome. I mean, I know it must be shock for us to be together so quickly. But I guess when you know, you just know." Jo said beaming from ear to ear.

Holding back a groan, Beth smiled at her friend. Fake it till you make it time. "I guess so. He isn't really the girlfriend type, so yes, it is a bit of a shock. But hey, if you feel you know someone well enough after only knowing them a few days, I'm happy for you. Now let's talk

Direct, Explicit Instruction because I for one am glad to be on time for this class."

"What? That's all I get? No steamy details about you and my cousin? It has moved pretty quick for the both of you, too hasn't it? That party was truly a great night. It bought us both a boyfriend!" Jo squealed as she wrapped her arms around a white as a ghost Beth.

Was this true? Corey had kissed her. He had hinted at spending more time with her. But surely, she would know if she was going out with someone? The attention was nice and all, but she didn't know him at all. And that kiss. That had not left a great impression. "I think you are getting a little ahead of yourself there Jo. Corey was nice to me but I am sure he has other girls to think about."

"Are you kidding? He has been texting me and asking me questions about you. He wants me to set up a dinner with you tomorrow? Can I give him your number?"

"I, ah, I guess so? I can't do tomorrow though. Pizza Tuesday. Matthew, Lori and I always spend Pizza Tuesday together. We promised no matter what happens, we will all still get together at least once a week. I guess I will need to go pick Matthew up, but I will organise that when I see him this afternoon." Beth replied as politely as she could.

"Oh, are you going to see him are you? I was going to skip my afternoon lecture and see him. I mean, we haven't had that much alone time together, and I like the idea of finishing off that sponge bath in a naughty nurse kind of way." Jo said in a flirty voice.

"Sorry? Are you actually asking me NOT to go and see my best friend so you can throw yourself at him? You do realise he has two broken ribs and a fractured ankle right? Did the whole trip to the hospital skip your mind?" Beth fumed. She could not believe it. This girl, she had known for only seven days, was trying to keep her away from Matthew? Who the hell did she think she was? Not able to take any more of the conversation, Beth stepped away from Jo and made her way into the room.

Sitting down deliberately amongst the other students so there was no room for the other girl, Beth glanced at her phone. Opening the text, she smiled at Matthew's response. *"Love M, xx"*. Don't analyse it, she told herself. You tell each other you love them all the time. Had he ever sent kisses before though? Get out of your head girl! Focus. But he would expect a response.

"At some point you will need to get used to me not being around. For now, you're stuck with me. Have a boring day! Love Beth xx".

Short, playful. Everything she was not feeling as she thought about the girl who was going to be getting those kisses rather than her. His response was almost immediate.

"Don't ever say that to me again. You are always mine. And can you stop for some M&M's on your way. I am sure they will make me feel better. Love you more, M xxx".

Deciding it was for the best, Beth sent him a message back. It was disappointing, but no way did she feel like getting involved with his love life. Especially if she had to witness them kissing. *"Can't do it sorry. Will see what I can do about the M&M's. How's the ribs? Love B xxx"*

Thirty seconds later the reply sounded out in the suddenly quiet theatre. Cursing herself and switching it to silent, Beth opened the screen and had to chuckle. *"They need kissing better. And what does it mean – You can't do it sorry? You not coming to see me? Don't break my heart Bethy. Love M xxxx"*.

This had to stop. He couldn't flirt with her like this. It would tear her apart. *"Matthew James, stop being such a flirt. Your girlfriend is coming over after lunch apparently. She will help with the kissing part. Not sure about the M&M's. Don't overdo it. Be good, if you know what that means, Love Beth xxxx"*.

It was towards the end of the lecture, that Beth could remember nothing from, that his reply came. *"Still trying to work out how I have a girlfriend. What if I want you instead? See you soon please? Love you most, Matthew xxxxx"*.

Beth couldn't breathe. It doesn't mean what you think it means she told herself. He means, he wants you to come over today. He really just wants his chocolate. She could be nice and tell Jo to take some. But Beth wasn't feeling very charitable in that moment. Re-reading the message,

Beth had no idea how to answer. She had a break after the tutorial class and she would sit and find the words to say to him after that. *Love you most...* a simple poem from their childhood.

I love you –
I love you more-
I love you most –
I love you to the moon and back-
I love you to the moon and back a hundred million times –
You win –
We both win.

She didn't feel like she was winning right now though. When a text came through Beth almost jumped out of her skin in anticipation. It was from Corey. OK. Looked like they were all going to Pizza Tuesday. It felt like it was so out of Beth's control. This was not what she wanted. But what was the point in fighting it? At least she had someone paying her attention right? Sending an *"O.K sounds great!"* to Corey, and a *"Company for pizza tomorrow- sorry"* to Lori, Beth sent one last text as she went back to her studies. *"Can you bring Matthew to Pizza tomorrow night please? Corey and I will meet you there."*

The response from Jo was lightening *"Of course! So happy. Just like a double date! I will give him a kiss for you when I get there. Just about to leave now – Jo x".*

Like a kick to the guts, Beth turned her phone off and was determined to throw herself into her assignments. It wasn't until she was almost home that she remembered to turn her phone back on. What do you know. Three missed calls from Matthew. Torn between wondering if he was ok, and wanting to forget all about him, Beth sent a simple text before she started working on dinner. Lori had offered, but Beth was determined to make life as easy as possible for Lori until she was back to 100%.

"Love you to the moon and back – Love Beth xxxxxx"

She wasn't expecting a response. She refused to keep checking her phone. After the steak and salad was demolished, and the dishes were done, Beth settled on her bed to read. Lori had said little about her day, but she suspected Lori had been in contact with Joshua again. Weird. Not the most likely of friends happening there, but I Beth could not see any danger in it. He seemed a bit of a loser for Lori to be wasting time on though. Not her usual class of friends.

Just before shutting her phone off and charging it for the night, Beth checked the screen. When did that message come in? Must have been when she went to the bathroom. Punching in her unlock code, Beth already knew what it would say. And she was right. Simple words, used many times over the years but more meaningful and more painful than they had ever been.

"Goodnight my Beth. I love you to the moon and back a hundred million times – Matthew xxxxxxx".

With a sigh, Beth shut the phone down and forced herself to calm down. Sleep took forever to come. A restless night filled with questions and concerns.

CHAPTER 21

Josh opened the door and had to smirk. So, this was the chick making waves. Not that she wasn't ok to look at. She just seemed to be missing something. Before he got a chance to invite her in, the girl stepped up to him and gave him a hug.

"Matthew never told me he had a brother. You're his brother, right? You look so much alike. I'm Jo. I'm not normally good at meeting people but I guess because I'm going out with your brother I feel comfortable with you" Jo said and Joshua wondered if she always talked that fast.

"Ahhh, Hi, yeah, I'm Josh. Older, wiser brother. Not surprised he didn't mention me, not like you have known each other that long. He didn't mention you either. Beth's the only girl of his we have ever talked about" Josh added that last bit in, hoping it would sting a bit. It seemed to work.

"Well, there is plenty of time for that." Jo said as she stepped into the house and made her way to the bedroom.

Matthew was well aware he had a visitor, and he also had a feeling he wasn't going to like who it was. He had about a minute to decide how to play this. With books all around him, it would be easy to say he was too busy for visitors. It's not that there was anything wrong with Jo. She was an ok girl. Just not his girl. She wasn't Beth and faking it just didn't seem possible anymore.

When Jo walked into the room, Matthew pretended to be asleep again. Joshua had other plans for his little bro though, and knocked loudly on the door, making enough noise that it was impossible to be asleep. Giving the obligatory stretch and yawn, Matthew won an Oscar for his 'just waking up' performance and when Jo came in to hug him, he took the chance to glare at his brother across the room. What a brat.

"Beth has asked me to bring you to pizza tomorrow. She can't get here because my cousin wants to spend time with her before we go out. Isn't that great? A double date! She told me that her flatmate and you and her always have dinner together on a Tuesday? That's so sweet. I guess I will have to try and change some shifts at work so I can come with you. Lucky for you I called in sick this week." Jo told him, seating herself on the edge of the bed.

Removing some books from under her, Matthew was a little hurt. It had always been the three of them for Pizza Tuesdays. And it looked like they were being invaded. A double date? His idea of torture. But at least he could make sure that meathead kept his hands off his girl. Since when did she become his girl? Well ok, in his mind she was, but now he was thinking it freely? Almost like admitting it to his brother had made it true.

Smiling and nodding through the conversation, hoping it was in the right places, Matthew kept checking his phone. His last message to Beth had been pretty bold ... *What if I want you instead? See you soon please? Love you most, Matthew xxxxx*".

He had a little smile when he counted the kisses. They seem to be growing. But that was about 40 minutes ago and no response. Telling himself it was because she was in class, Matthew tried his best to be attentive to his visitor. He sat through her making him a sandwich despite not being hungry and it being way after lunchtime. He suggested they watch some TV, in the hope that she would get bored or at least stop talking. As they flicked through the afternoon viewing, a movie caught Jo's eye. Love, Rosie was playing. And although he cringed at the idea of a chick flick, he relented and decided he could actually sleep.

Jo went out to the kitchen to make popcorn and as she did, Beth's text came through. It stopped his heart. He couldn't take too much more of this. He felt like he was an addict waiting for his next hit.

"Love you to the moon and back – Love Beth xxxxxx"

A simple enough message, with oh so much potential. And an extra kiss! Matthew couldn't keep the smile off his face, but before he could reply, Jo returned with the bowl. She noticed his smile and apparently attributed it to her own actions as she herself looked very pleased as she handed him the bowl. The silence plan worked. She snuggled up to him until he complained about the ribs, and they settled down to watch the afternoon movie.

Matthew wasn't sure how much they had missed but the plot of the movie grabbed his attention at some point. Best friends, always going out with other people but probably in love with each other? The irony of the movie was not lost on him. At least it had a happy ending. But if he had to wait that long to be with Beth he would probably go insane. Or combust from sexual frustration. And that was saying something because he was finding it hard – so to speak – to turn Jo's advances down. When a girl grabs your crotch and offers to blow your mind, you are probably out of your mind to say no. But he did.

Kissing her briefly goodbye, Matthew had no idea how to end this with her. But it must end. Maybe when she dropped him home tomorrow? Then he could focus his attention on getting that dufus out of Beth's life so he could move in. Move in. In more ways than one. Remembering he hadn't replied to Beth's earlier message, Matthew was happy with his retort. *MY BETH.* That's what she was to him. Now just to find a way to make that happen.

As Josh came in to help him to the John, Matthew was amazed at how good his brother had been the last few days.

"I appreciate this you know bro? I am actually really happy that you have been here or all this shit would be really hard." Matthew said genuinely meaning it.

"Ha, no worries. Didn't want you to have to whip that thing out with that girl here, she might have thought it was a proposal or something!" Joshua shouted from outside the toilet door.

"Please don't remind me! I am in need of a way out of that one." Matthew said as he limped out of the loo and into the bathroom to wash his hands. Joshua helped him in an awkward hug type manoeuvre that didn't put too much pressure on the ribs. As they made slow progress back to the bedroom, something occurred to Matthew. "Where is mum? And Douche bag? I thought for sure he would have been on the couch drinking beers by now. Did mum even come home last night?"

"Are you serious? Do you not even know?" Joshua said shaking his head in disbelief.

"Do I fucking look like I know, tell me ok? Where is our mother?" Matthew said starting to feel the worry build up.

"They're in Broome for a week. They left two days ago. How is it you don't know?"

"Huh, Broome. Nice of someone to tell me. No, I didn't know. And why are they there?" Matthew questioned.

"Keith got offered a few days' work there. He told mum to pack a bag and have a holiday while he was there. So, if you had no idea where she was, she probably has no idea you are injured either? I wonder how we can get in touch with her?" Joshua said as he helped Matthew into the bed.

"No, don't worry. I'm happy for her. She deserves a break. If we tell her she will just come racing back here and worry about me. I'm just really surprised. And it was Keith's idea for her to have a holiday?" Matthew wondered out loud.

"Yeah it was. At first I thought it was just cos he was too lazy to cook his own meals and stuff, but I heard him talking to her before they left. He reminded her to bring a few of her sloppy romance books so she could relax and read on the beach. I almost fell out of my chair. Seems to be on the level."

Well, wasn't that just a miracle Matthew thought to himself. First Joshua turns into a human being and holds a full conversation with him, and now Keith is working and taking Mum on a holiday? Saying goodnight to Josh, Matthew wondered what other miracles were in store for tomorrow.

CHAPTER 22

Lori was awake and even contemplating returning to classes. But was that out of habit or want. The course she was on may not be her lifelong dream, but Beth was right. She wasn't a quitter. Lori pulled her laptop over from its bag on the floor and fired it up. Cringing at the amount of emails, she started sorting through them. It was kind of surprising that most of them seemed to know of her hospital stay. But not that surprising really, when you had a friend like Bethany Holden.

After forty minutes of trashing unwanted mail, Lori made herself a grid. *Assignments Due, Readings needed, and What have I missed.* Printing a page out for each unit with the appropriate title, Lori double checked her timetable. Nothing holding her back really. Maybe one or two classes today. She could always come home. No one seemed to be too pissed about her absence so far.

Noticing that Beth was still asleep, Lori quietly made her way to the bathroom to prepare for the day. She wasn't dreading it as much as she had been. The difference she figured was how she was now looking at her course. It was no longer a dead-end path to something she did not want to do. Thanks to Beth, Lori was looking past the course to what could happen afterwards. It was like that Meme on Facebook with two dogs standing in mud. One short, and covered up to his face. The other tall and only covered up to his paws. The depth is the same, it's your perspective that changes.

Before leaving, Lori boiled the kettle and made a cuppa for Beth. Placing it next to the bed, Lori gently shook Beth awake. Unsure of the girls' class schedule, it was better safe than sorry. Beth seemed shocked at what she saw in front of her. Before her friend could try and stop her, Lori rushed out the door with a yell of "Cuppa's on the bedside for you, have a great day!".

Wiping the sleep out of her eyes, Beth tried to remember the dream she was just having. Whatever it was had left her warm and tingling on the inside. And where the hell did Lori think she was going? Sitting up, Beth took the cup and drank a healthy amount, grateful for the gesture. The only person that usually makes her a morning cuppa is Matthew.

Feeling positive about the day ahead and having no idea why, Beth took her time choosing her clothes. Great classes today with a nice early finish, dinner with her friends and a possible love interest. It was going to be great. Standing in front of her wardrobe, Beth scanned the rack for fifteen minutes to no avail.

A little frustrated now, Beth just couldn't decide what to wear. Nothing she had went with her feeling of wanting to hide her tummy. She was in that mood of wanting glamour, but feeling like wearing a tent. There were plenty of days when Beth felt the need to cover herself. Wear ultra-baggy clothes that hid all her bumps. Today was that day.

Slumping to the floor, Beth knew she was being unreasonable. Her logical brain told her that she was no bigger or smaller than the day before. But her emotional brain was having none of the rational talk. People always assumed because she was friendly and generally happy in front of people, that she was doing ok mentally. In truth, it had been pointed out to her by Lori, that Beth's need to care for everyone was her way of over compensating for her poor self-esteem. She didn't deny it.

"Ahhhhhhh, damn it!" Beth cursed as she looked down at her pyjama clad body. Just pick something she thought to herself. Closing her eyes and sticking her hand in, Beth pulled out a skirt and decided to just go with it. She could wear tights to keep warm, and let's face it, if Corey didn't like her he wouldn't have invited himself tonight.

Unsatisfied with her appearance but resigned to life as a bigger girl,

Beth left for Uni in plenty of time despite the twenty-five-minute delay in choosing her outfit. Sending a quick text to Lori, asking if she was coming to pizza tonight, Beth wrestled with whether to text Matthew as well. Why should she not text her friend? This was not right she thought to herself. No-one should stop her contacting her friend if she wanted to. How had she let this new person in her life control her time with her best friend of fourteen years?

Beth opened her message screen again as she sat down in the lecture theatre.

"*Good Morning sunshine. Hope you are being a good boy and resting. I will see you tonight. Love Beth x*".

She hit send and then cursed herself. She sent another one off straight away.

"*I win x*".

Smiling to herself, she turned it to silent and looked around the room. Jo was approaching and Beth smiled at her, deliberately working hard to smooth things over. The was no sane reason for Beth to be annoyed at Matthew. Matthew was not really hers even if she did want him. Beth been through this many times before and she would get through it again. She told herself this over and over and over as Jo continued to talk about her time with "Matty" as she called him.

Beth smiled secretly to herself knowing Matthew would not like that nickname. There was a boy at school with them called Matty Lilywhite, who everyone said smelled like wee. He was one of those unfortunate kids that no one liked and Bethany was the only one who ever made an effort with him. He was chubby, often dirty and deadly shy. Matthew James was not impressed to share a name with him and was happy when Beth started calling him "Hue" as a joke.

All day Beth waited for a response from her Hue. She had received one from Lori saying she didn't want to intrude on the double date. Beth quickly set her straight with that and insisted she come so she could meet Corey and give her opinion. But nada from the boy. Even Cory had messaged checking the location and sending way too many kisses in a text to someone he only just met.

Arriving at the restaurant before anyone else, Beth struggled with the 'where to sit?' dilemma. She didn't want to be boxed in and not be able to get in and out. And Matthew would need lots of space for his moon boot. Completely flabbergasted with the situation and lost in the moment of despair, Beth let out a squeal as a paper aeroplane flew over her head and landed on the table in front of her.

Whirling around, Beth knew he was here. She hadn't realised how much she had missed his gorgeous face. Well maybe she had but she was trying to deny it. The smile he wore was worth a million bucks. Dressed in jeans that had been cut up one leg to make way for the cast, and a wrinkled but perfect fitting green shirt, with rolled up sleeves, Matthew looked effortlessly sexy. Snatching up the paper plane, Beth turned away from his hotness and opened up the note. Three words. *"We both win."*

Chuckling to herself, she watched her seriously good-looking friend limp towards her slowly but couldn't wait any longer. She raced towards him, stopping herself from squeezing him hard. "Nice throw" Beth said as she leaned in and gently embraced Matthew. "How's the ribs?".

"Better now I have my Beth with me. How could you leave me alone for two whole days with nothing to do?" Matthew said quietly for just the two of them to hear. Before she could answer Jo infused herself between them and almost pushed Mathew into a seat at the table. "Easy there Jo, I'm not completely helpless." Matthew said visibly trying to keep calm.

Sitting herself next to Matthew, Beth was happy to see him. Her mood all day was unsettled, frustrated and just not right after the clothes debarkle. With him by her side, she felt calmer, happier and almost taller in a way. How can one person have that much effect on you she thought to herself. Matthew nudged her arm indicating she had missed something somewhere.

"Huh?" was her oh so intelligent response.

"I said, what have you been doing all day? Because you smell nice." Matthew leaned towards her putting his head on her shoulder.

Without realising it, Beth had put on Matthew's favourite perfume of hers. He was with her when she bought it and said it reminded him of her mum's cookies. Usually saving it for special occasions, Beth had put it on unconsciously this morning. "Thanks, you smell better than you did last time I saw you. I guess your personal nurse is doing a good job then. You don't need me after all." Beth said smiling at him.

"Actually, my brother has been helping me. Didn't think I could risk taking my clothes off around any of the ladies, I know how you all feel about my irresistible body!" Matthew said winking at Beth.

Jo was still settling in to her seat, having adjusted her low-cut, slim fitting dress a few times to the best vantage point for Matthew. She has clearly gone all out with her preparations tonight. Hair perfectly styled in that shiny and straight manner that Beth could never achieve. Full makeup and kilos of jewellery adorning her body. Matthew shook his head and whispered to Beth "Let's face it, you girls would sell your souls for a look at me naked."

Beth couldn't help but laugh. He was so full of himself. But of course, he was right. "Speaking of your body, show me your ribs Hue, has the bruising gone down any?" she asked as she began to lift his shirt, a slight blush touching her cheeks. Matthew breathed in deep with pleasure, as Beth's knuckles swept across his skin.

"Trying to undress another man, I might get jealous Bethany" came the deep, loud drawl from across the room.

CHAPTER 23

Embarrassed and completely aware she was blushing like a tomato, Beth drew her hands back and turned towards the voice. Corey was dressed in a bright t-shirt and cargo shorts. It was obvious his clothes were ironed and also very new. He was striking in appearance, chiselled some might say, but even though Beth acknowledged that thought, the boy sitting next to her was still the sexiest man she had ever seen.

Standing to greet Corey, he pulled Beth in for a hug and then kissed her deeply. Coughing, Matthew interrupted loudly "Nice to see you again man, forgive me for not getting up. That's one hell of a greeting. Do I get a kiss too?"

Beth giggled and took the time to retake her seat and calm her beating heart. Taking up residence on Beth's other side, Corey almost ignored Matthew and hardly greeted his cousin.

"What can I get you to drink babe? I'm having a beer, you want a wine or something?" Corey asked her, looking straight into her eyes.

"I, um, I'm ok thanks. I will just have water later. But thank you, really, that is sweet of you. Actually, can you please get Matthew a beer too? I was just going to get him one." Beth questioned.

"Oh, I'll get it." Jo jumped in rising from her chair, still fidgeting with her dress.

"Great, let's head to the bar then cuz." Corey said as he moved away, brushing his hand over Beth's shoulders as he left.

"Well, he is friendly. Not entirely sure how I feel about him with his hands all over you though. What do we even know about him?" Matthew said when they were alone.

"Who cares when he looks like that, and kisses like that, personality doesn't really matter does it?" Beth said half joking to tease her friend.

Matthew did not like that answer. He knew Beth was joking but to hear her talk about someone else as good looking. Damn it. She should only be looking at him, not some blonde, steroid using, sleaze bag. "Bethy baby, am I not your favourite eye candy anymore? Please tell me it's not true." Matthew joked trying to ease the pain in his head.

"Well I'm sorry Matthew, but there are certain needs I require that you my friend cannot meet" Beth replied, half watching Corey and Jo at the bar, and half watching the door for Lori to arrive.

Tugging on her arm to gain her attention, Matthew looked deep into those stunning blue eyes and said, "What needs would those be baby girl?"

The silence between them stretched on. Beth held his gaze while she pondered her answer. She should joke it off like she always did. But something in the way he was looking at her was making her insides boil. "Women have the same urges as men Hue. I might combust from frustration and loneliness soon. Finally, a good-looking man is paying attention to me, and I intend to do what needs to be done to get those needs met."

Matthew frowned. Did she actually mean she would sleep with this buffoon? "Why the hell would you waste your time on that walking hair do?" Matthew spat angrily.

Before Beth could reply, Lori entered the conversation. "This looks intense, should I leave you two to it?". Neither of them had heard Lori approach. And neither of them looked away from the eyes in front of them.

Snapping out of it first, Matthew put on a cheery fake smile and welcomed Lori. "Hi there Lori, I've missed you! We were just discussing Fabio over there with the perfectly combed and conditioned hair. Please, join us and tell us what you think of Beth's lover boy."

Lori had landed smack bang into a minefield. The sparks between these two could fuel the city's electricity for years. Matthew was not a happy camper. And Lori could tell it was not due to the ridiculous cast he wore on his injured leg. Something had to be done. Joshua and Lori had been colluding enough to know they both wanted each other. Anyone with half a brain could feel the tension in the air between them. Time to step up her efforts she thought. But how could she possibly get them to admit their feelings for each other.

With plans of handcuffs and locking them in the flat together going through her head, Lori looked up as two people approached. So, this was the thorn in Matthew's side. Not bad. And this other person must be the famous Jo. Hadn't Joshua said she was kind of pretty? Strange, Lori thought as she noticed the wide smile on the boy's face.

"Hello there, lovely lady. Please tell me you are here to join us?" Cory crooned.

Lori blinked, taken aback by the flirty and forward comment from a stranger. A stranger that was supposedly interested in her friend. And that is when she knew what she had to do. Beth wouldn't be happy with it at first, but afterwards she would see it was for the best. Lori fluttered her eyelids and positioned herself seductively as she introduced herself. "It's your lucky day cowboy. I'm Lori and this is my regular table. So if YOU are a good boy, I might even let you stay."

Seeing the confused look on Beth's face, Lori turned away and found a seat at the table. It did not escape her notice that Matthew looked positively seething. It would work better if they all thought this was for real. Corey sat himself down between Beth and herself, but angled his body towards hers. Jo, seemingly unaware of the tension at the table, gave a cheery greeting, introducing herself to Lori and complimenting her on her outfit. The tight fitting black jeans and silk shirt were nothing too special, but Lori did know they fit her well.

Blondy seemed to like her outfit too. In fact, he almost looked like he was drooling. "Do you have a name cowboy, or should I just call you that all night?" Lori said seductively.

Corey appeared tongue tied. This over confident, arrogant, and over muscled man could hardly speak Beth thought. "Lori, this is Corey, the one I was telling you about. He is pretty special isn't he?" Beth emphasised, trying to infer the 'he is mine.'

Corey finally found his voice. "Yes, I'm Corey, but it sounds like you girls have been talking about me hey? Did Beth tell you how good looking I am, or did her description not do me justice?"

Matthew suddenly seemed to choke on his beer. Really, what was his problem? It was most likely something he would say. Beth tried to steer the conversation towards the menu. "Well, shall we order? I'm starving!"

"What's the hurry Bethany? Your lovely friend here has just arrived. I for one would like to get to know her better, and give her a chance to look at the menu" Corey said, not taking his eyes off Lori.

"Oh, I already know what I want." Lori said dramatically, before adding "I do come here every week after all. I'm going to go and order."

"I'll come with you" Corey said jumping up to follow. He took two steps before turning to Beth and seemingly remembering he was on a date with her. "What can I get you Bethany? A salad or something?"

"Uhhh, no thanks, I will be over in a minute. I usually have pizza on Pizza Tuesdays. You go ahead though." Beth said feeling unsure of the whole situation. Should she have salad? That's what girls did when they went out with boys wasn't it? Tried to make it look like they ate well and took care of themselves?

"OK" he said and hurried off to the retreating Lori.

Turning to Matthew, Beth saw him shaking his head. "What's up with you? Feeling ok?"

"Am I feeling OK? That idiot is falling all over himself trying to impress Lori, and then offers you a salad? What kind of date is that?" Matthew fumed.

"I always have a salad" Jo said, making Matthew put his head in his hands and laugh.

"Well that proves it. He is definitely not the right man for you Beth. He doesn't know you at all. A real man would offer you the menu and say order one of everything, what-ever you like my Princess" Matthew said, still laughing.

"Should I order for you then Prince Charming?" Beth said feeling somewhere in between amused and confused.

"I can do it for him. You don't have to do it all for him Beth, he has a girlfriend now" Jo said firmly.

"Actually, she does have to order for me because we always share. And since you only eat rabbit food, I need a girl in my life that knows how I like my pizza." Matthew stated looking directly at Beth as he said it.

"Oh, OK, can you order me a Caesar salad then too please Beth and I will pay you back after. That way Matty and I can have some alone time with you gone" Jo said, cuddling up to Matthew.

"First, don't call me Matty, it reminds me of urine, and two, where did this girlfriend stuff come from? At what point did I ever ask you to be my girlfriend?" Matthew stated.

Beth did not wait around to hear the answer to that! Definitely her cue to leave. As she walked towards the counter she saw Corey and Lori up ahead. They were standing very close together for two people that had just met. As Beth stepped up behind them, she heard Corey say in Lori's ear "You are so sexy, the only thing on the menu I want to order is you."

CHAPTER 24

Dropping her purse with a loud clang, Beth fought back the tears. She had no right to him. They weren't together officially. But wow did it hurt. Of course he would want Lori. Beth could never compare to her. As they turned to look at what had made the noise, Beth avoided eye contact. She simply picked up her purse and turned to go. She had no intention of letting them see her upset. Corey had other plans though.

"Beth, you ready to order? Lori and I were just trying to decide what we wanted. Lori is a bad influence, she wants to order dessert first."

Still avoiding his eyes, Beth wondered why he was still pretending. She had a choice. Go quietly into the night and fade away like she normally would when faced with an asshole, or call him on his bullshit. Who was she kidding? This guy needed to be told.

"You fucking sleazy bastard! You kiss me, and come here to see me, and then as soon as she turns up, you dribble all over yourself looking at her. Well, you can have her. You lost your chance with me, and you! So, girl code means nothing to you? You knew how I felt about him. You know how hard it is for me to find anyone to take an interest. I think you like me being the only virgin in Australia! You can have any one you want. Don't bother coming home tonight. I don't care where you go, but it isn't there. I don't think I can ever forgive you for this."

And with that, Beth turned and made her way back to the table to retrieve her bag. The tears were flowing freely now but she didn't care. People were staring at her, after her very loud confessions, but Beth didn't care. By the time she reached the table, it was clear that Jo and Matthew were not having a good night either. Jo was crying and Matthew was doing his best to soothe her without getting too close to her physically.

Matthew looked up in relief when Beth approached, obviously thankful back up had arrived. His relief turned immediately to anger when he saw his girl crying. "What has happened?" Matthew said breaking contact with a sobbing Jo. Standing up as best he could, he watched as Beth tried to hide her face. She was collecting her bag. "Bethany Holden, tell me what has happened and who had made you cry so I can go and punch them in the face!".

The statement forced Jo's head up and ceased her crying. It also elicited a hysterical giggle out of Bethany. "I don't think you are in any shape to do that Hue, but thank you for the gesture. I just need to get out of here. I'll see you later OK, sorry." Beth said as she started to walk away.

Matthew called after her, "Wait, I'm coming with you."

Saying a quick and awkward goodbye to Jo, Matthew limp/fast walked to Beth, who had paused to wait for him, still crying and noticing the stares. Matthew began to question her, but Beth stopped him with a hand up. "No, not here, I'm already a mess and I just want to go home. If I stay any longer I will punch someone myself."

The ride in the car was quiet apart from Beth's light sobs and her occasional blowing of her nose. Matthew was tense and alert in the passenger seat, feeling like he needed to tear someone's head off for making Beth so upset. He had a feeling he knew what the problem was. He had seen himself, the way that dick Corey had been looking at Lori. And it's not as if Lori helped the matter the way she was talking to him. Fuck. If that was it, then he could relax. That guy was never good enough for his Beth anyway. No one ever would be.

Sensing Matthew's questioning glare, Beth didn't know where to start. "I'm OK Hue. I just needed to get out of there. As you could probably tell, Corey is not as interested in me as I had thought he was. He just didn't show it in the best way is all."

Helping Matthew out of the car, Beth had calmed herself down to some degree. "Thanks Bethy, I know this sucks having to help me when you are upset."

Reaching the apartment, Beth threw herself down on her bed and couldn't hold back the tears that came anew. Closing the front door and locking up, Matthew hobbled around the apartment and made them both a cup of hot chocolate. Taking one cup in at a time, Matthew sat on the end of the bed before finally speaking. "Beth, come on darling, talk to me. There has to be more that is upsetting you than just that idiot. Tell me what's wrong?"

"I know you didn't like him Hue, but when was the last time I had a boyfriend? And I know he wasn't my boyfriend, and I know that he only kissed me a few times. But he danced with me, and held me, and made me feel like I might have a chance to be intimate with someone. I need it. I need to feel like someone knows me inside and out. I crave it. I feel like I'm only half a person, never having experienced what it is like to have passion and all those deep emotions when you are in love with someone and you can't get enough of them. I'm sick of being everyone's friend. I hate my body and the way I am right now. I feel like I will never have anyone who wants me like that. Just because I have a bigger body and I'm not as interesting or glamorous as the bimbos that walk around, doesn't mean I don't have my own needs. I want attention, and Corey was the first person to give that to me in a very long time."

Matthew had stayed silent through the ranting. He hated hearing her talk about herself like that. A bigger girl? What made Beth amazing was nothing to do with her body, but her plentiful body was a bonus in Matthew's opinion. And this talk actually pissed him off.

"So you're telling me you were willing to put up with that guy, just because he gave you some attention, even though you know he was a dick? That's what your telling me Beth? Cos' fuck I thought you were smarter than that!" Matthew said firmly as he began to pace wobblily around the bedroom.

"You don't get it Hue. How could you? You are gorgeous. Women throw themselves at you. You have had more women than I have had beers, and you have this ability to not get attached. You get all the attention you want and sometimes don't want so the concept that someone could feel invisible around you is too foreign for you to understand." Beth shouted back feeling frustrated with him and all the world.

"What the hell are you talking about? Beth, you are far from invisible. You are the most amazing girl I have ever known. You. You are so wrong about this. You are the one that doesn't get it. It has nothing to do with what you do or don't look like. It's more than that. You are more than that. You are sweet, and funny and the most stubborn and determined person in the world. Well, apart from me that is. You put up with all my bullshit and still find time to make everyone feel better about themselves. You inspire us all to be better, do better. And you are so god damn sexy you make my brain explode."

As the words left Matthews' mouth he felt lighter. Instantly, he knew, it was what he had needed to say for a long time. Without realising it, they had moved so they were facing each other across the room. When did she get off the bed? Matthew had been so caught up in admitting how he felt he hadn't noticed her move. And the silence in the room as they stared at each other was like a thick wall between them. Matthew had thought he had said enough. He needed her to respond. In fact, if she didn't respond soon, he was going to have a stroke.

The expression on Beth's face gave nothing away. Was she even breathing? Matthew didn't think he was. He didn't need oxygen anyway. What he needed was standing in front of him. And then, without warning, Beth's response was physical rather than verbal. She sped forward and kissed Matthew full on the lips. The heat between them, and the softness of her lips on his stopped his brain from functioning. At this point he couldn't even tell you what his name was. All he knew, was that the girl of his dreams was kissing him, and man it felt good.

CHAPTER 25

Not to be outdone, Matthew took control of the situation and kissed Beth back with everything he had. This was not a drill! Time for giving it his all. Pulling Beth closer, he balanced on his good leg and wrapped his arms around her perfect body. They fit together so well he thought, as she moved her hands to his chest and then, slipping them around to his bum. Time for air Matthew thought as he gasped at her touch.

Thinking she had done something wrong, Beth dropped her hands and stepped away. "Sorry" was all she said, keeping her eyes on the floor between them.

"What the hell for?" Matthew said out of breath and unbelievably happy.

"I, um, I'm sorry for kissing you. I understand…" Matthew cut Beth off with his mouth on hers and this time he snaked his hands around to her backside and squeezed.

"Let me tell you this once, and I never want to have to say it again OK?" Matthew said, bringing Beth's face up to meet his eyes. "Never, ever, in my lifetime, apologise for kissing me. Got that? In fact, you should really say sorry for not kissing me. It has taken us long enough." Matthew said affectionately while running his hands through her hair.

"I feel so, I don't know, I… I have been in love with you so long, I feel like this can't possibly be real." Beth admitted, still in Matthews arms.

"You have? Really? Wow. I need to sit down." Matthew said, dragging Beth with him as he wobbled to the bed.

"Oh shit, sorry, I, um, was I little too forceful there? Did I hurt your ribs? Shit, I will get you some ice or something, do you need pain killers? Tell me what I can…"

"Beth, it's fine, come and sit with me. You didn't hurt me. In fact, I think you just made everything better."

"You can't mean that Matthew. In the state you are in, you should be resting, not trying to make hysterical girls feel better." Beth sighed.

"Ha" Matthew let out a short laugh. "You think this is about making you feel better? You know me better than that Bethy. I am self-serving all the way. This, between us, is everything I have wanted for a very long time. I just never thought I deserved you. No, don't interrupt. You have done so much for me my whole life. And I will never feel like anyone is good enough for you. But I really want to keep trying to deserve you. You are so amazing, and I love you so much and shit, I've never said that to anyone before and meant it like I do now. But I love you Bethany, and I always will."

"It doesn't make sense. I just can't understand how you can say that with it being me, the way I am. You have never dated anyone even remotely bigger than a size 8 and you are telling me, you love me? Like, really want to be more than my friend? Because if you are joking with me I don't think I can take it Matthew."

"See, you keep saying things like that, and I get annoyed with you. I love you, but you are ridiculous. You want me to prove how I feel about your body? Here, is this proof enough?" Matthew said as he lifted Beth's hand and placed it on his very stiff groin.

Beth was shocked but very pleased. As a shy smile spread across her face, she felt such a wave of lust hit her and Matthew must have felt the same. Colliding together they kissed again, falling awkwardly on the bed they had been sitting on. Manoeuvring around Matthews broken ankle and his damaged ribs, they grabbed at each other hungrily, almost like they were using Braille to memorise each other's bodies.

But Matthew needed to put the brakes on. No way was he taking this further without some serious things being sorted.

"Beth, wait." Matthew said, forcing himself to stop the movement of his hands across her hips. "I just want to make this perfectly clear to you, and I need to hear something myself. There is no one else for me. I want you so damn much, but I couldn't handle it to watch you be with anyone else. Before we take this any further, tell me you are mine, and only mine. Please."

Beth felt tears in her eyes for the thousandth time that day. But this time they were happy tears. Feeling a little frustrated at the stop in the petting action, Beth decided to enjoy the moment and tease him. "Why Matthew James, are you asking me to be your girlfriend?" Beth said with a cheeky grin.

"You bet your fine ass I am." Matthew chuckled at her flirty response. And rather than give him a 'yes', she kissed him again.

The rushed hunger was gone now, and they laid down staring at each other, smiling. Matthew started with his hand running through Beth's hair. He grabbed the back of her neck and pulled her forward for a leisurely kiss. Pulling back, he traced the outline of her jaw with his thumb, caressing the lips he had just kissed and kept moving his palm down to her shoulder. Moving his fingers slowly over her arms and around to her front, Matthew felt his erection tighten. Gliding his fingers over her breasts, cupping each one in turn, Matthew could only imagine how hard he would get when he actually saw them.

As if reading his mind, Beth shifted herself slightly, and took off her shirt. Matthew's jaw dropped. His erection did not. The most amazing breasts, wrapped in delicate black silk were in front of him. Almost shaking, he traced the line of silk across the top of the bra. "You are so beautiful." Matthew breathed as he took in every inch of Beth he could see. Beth giggled as Matthew trailed down her ribs and laid his large palm across her stomach.

Sucking her stomach in, Beth felt ashamed of her flesh. In in the back of her mind she was waiting for Matthew to turn away, tell her he didn't like what he saw. But as he did see, and he did touch, Beth lost her inhibitions and enjoyed the moment. Sitting up a little, Beth leaned across the gorgeous boy in front of her, and began lifting his shirt. She needed to see him and feel him like he was doing to her.

As they lay there, both shirtless, speechless and completely addicted to the feel of their skin under their hands, Beth, for the first time ever, felt truly beautiful. It wasn't his words that made her feel that way. It was his gaze that seared through her, clearly liking what he saw. They kissed again, a deep lingering kiss that was different from the others. And the next was just as special again, as the kisses grew deeper and more forceful.

Pressing into each other, fitting together in all the right places, Beth's soft parts against the firmness of Matthews fit body, the sizzling between Beth's legs spiked into volcano territory. But as Matthew moved his body over hers, he winced in pain from the pesky ribs that had been damaged. And damn, wasn't that a cold shower into proceedings. "Wait!" Beth said pulling herself out from under that fine body.

"We need to stop this Matthew. You are in pain. This isn't right." Beth said putting distance between them.

"It feels very right to me. Baby, come back over here." Matthew said with the sexy smirk that always made Beth combust.

Moving slowly over to the bed again, Beth sat next to where Matthew was, sprawled across the bed, low hung jeans, no shirt and the smile of a Cheshire Cat. "What are you smiling about Matthew James?"

"You. I am smiling at you Bethany Holden. You take my breath away. And watching you walk over to me, dressed, or rather not dressed like that, I feel so fucking happy." Matthew reached up and placed his hands on either side of Beth's face. He pulled her down and kissed her again, sliding his tongue in and enjoying the taste of her. But she was right. He could not do this properly in the state he was in. "As much as it kills me to say this baby girl, I think you are right. I want you so much, but I think we need to wait till this cast comes off and I can breathe without cursing."

CHAPTER 26

Returning their shirts to their bodies, Beth and Matthew made their way to the kitchen, holding hands. After pausing in the hall to kiss again. Shoving Matthew into a seat, Beth made them toasted sandwiches and they sat at the small table, thighs touching and goofy smiles on their faces. Eating toasties and sharing a can of coke, Beth and Matthew talked about the craziness they had left behind only an hour ago.

"And what did she say after he said that to her?" Matthew asked Beth, referring to the Lori and Corey dramatics.

"I don't know, I dropped my purse and that made them turn around. By that time, they knew I was there, and then that horrible, sleaze of a guy just kept talking to me as if he hadn't just propositioned my friend. I was so upset, but then I was just really angry at him. I let him have it. I think I even called him a sleazy bastard." Beth admitted.

Matthew smiled and squeezed Beth's hand. In fact, he had hardly let go of it since they had left the bedroom. "That's my girl. Tell him to shove it. But what I can't comment on is Lori. Now don't get me wrong, she's not our favourite person right now, but do we really know if she was involved. She was flirty as hell but she always is. I think you need to at least talk to her. Hear her side of the story."

"Wow. Matthew James, I never in a million years thought I would hear you defending that girl. You and Lori have been unpleasant to each other since, well, since you have known each other. Why the change of heart?"

Matthew leaned closer to Beth and drew in a deep breath. She was so close, smelling like vanilla and looking all dishevelled from their epic make out session. Sexy as hell. "How can I be too upset with her Beth. Look how my night ended up. In truth, she did me a favour."

"Seriously, Hue, she could have any man, why do you think she did that? He isn't exactly her type either." Beth said sadly.

"I think you need to talk to her. To me, it doesn't add up. But let's just forget about it tonight ok? Can we just make our way back in that blissful room and hold each other? No funny business. Just a lot more of this…." He said as he kissed her lightly on the neck "and definitely more of this…" as his lips met hers, "and maybe a little of this…" as Matthew stroked Beth's nipples through the soft material, making her gasp in pleasure.

"Stop trying to distract me, you sexy boy. You haven't told me what happened with you and Jo yet. I am guessing you told her that you don't have girlfriends…SHIT! You did, didn't you? What is she going to think now? We will have to keep it a secret. We can't tell anyone! What the hell will everyone say? I feel so shitty." Beth exclaimed.

"Relax, Beth. It's ok. Jo needed to be handled. It was getting out of control. I just asked her why she thought she was my girlfriend. I simply pointed out, that I had never asked her to be, and that was enough to set her off. I never claimed I didn't DO girlfriends, which is kind of great, because I have every intention of do-ing my girlfriend as soon as this cast is off." Matthew said with a devilish glint in his eye. "And as for not telling anyone. Fuck that. I want to tell everyone. I will write it on a billboard if I have to. You, Beth Holden are my girlfriend, and there is no way I am keeping that secret." With that, Matthew leaned forward and kissed her again. He would never tire of this. Matthew got lost in the feel of her on his mouth and the tingles she left on his skin.

Leaving the dishes on the table, and stopping to kiss every few metres, Beth and Matthew made their way to the bathroom. Brushing their teeth side by side, they giggled as they moved down the small hallway to the bedroom. They had done this a million times, but this was turning out to be the best so far. Who knew simply brushing your teeth with the man you loved would be so erotic?

Helping Matthew into bed, and then, making her own way in, Beth did not want to turn off the light. She was afraid she would wake up in the morning and this beautiful boy beside her would not be there. As if he could sense her worry, Matthew pulled himself closer and nuzzled her neck. Switching the lamp off, Beth turned to face Matthew. In the adjusting light, Beth could make out the lovely shape of his face, the curve of his luscious lips and the slight smirk he flashed.

"You look so serious Bethy, what's up?" Matthew said low and tantalisingly in her ear.

"I don't want to sleep. I don't want to risk this not being real." Beth admitted shyly.

"I know how you feel. I am unbelievably happy right now. I feel like I could run a marathon or wrestle a bear. You make me feel so friggin strong and good, I just can't believe how lucky I am. But I promise you, I am not going anywhere. Now that I have you, I am not letting you go. So, go to sleep. It's been a crazy ass day. And in the morning, you will see that this is real."

With that, Matthew kissed Beth softly and wrapped his body around hers the best he could. As he closed his eyes, he prayed that his ribs would heal fast so he could hold his girl tighter than he was now. As he started to drift off to sleep, he heard Beth whisper something. The fog of sleep was too thick for him to respond, but he knew it was ok. He would get the chance to say "I love you too" in the morning.

CHAPTER 27

A whole week went by without a word from Jo, Corey or Lori. Beth did notice some of Lori's clothes were missing though, so she just assumed Lori had been in while Beth was at Uni. While the absence was noted but not mourned, the addition to the apartment was truly welcomed. More of Matthews clothes were mixed in with Beth's now and after a perfect week of dating this sexy man, Beth was still pinching herself. And oh boy was it hard to not get lost in daydreams about him.

Slowly, Matthew had been getting used to getting around on his own without help, and his trip down to the local deli now, gave Beth some time dress up a bit before they went for pizza. They were determined to keep their routine up. This time, they would get a table for two though. Beth felt her heart flutter at the thought that she was going on a date with Matthew. Was it really a date though when they had done this so many times before?

Matthew arrived 5 mins later and limped over to his girl. He was getting used to the independence but he was hoping to get his body back soon as he was feeling less manly when his girl had to open the door for him, instead of the other way around. While he was away, Beth had changed into a sweet vintage style dress that showed off all her curves in the right places. Now that he had caved to his desire for her, he found it difficult to keep his hands off her.

Watching her flit across the room tidying up, Matthew took a deep breath. So, this is what happiness felt like? He knew it had only been a week, but in that week, he had tried desperately to catch up on the years of kisses they had missed. He had never taken his time with a girl before. Never before had he even wanted to. But he was enjoying the slow, irresistible build up that was happening between them.

Revealing himself into Beth's eyeline, Matthew felt like a million bucks when she hit him with her killer smile. "Hey baby, you like nice. But you'd look nice out of it too." He said with a sexy lift to his lips. Matthew prowled towards her and Beth stood motionless, watching him with pleasure in her eyes. But it was hard for him to look sexy when he was limping around, and Beth giggled at Matthews' slow pace and the wicked look in his eye.

"Down boy" Beth said as he got closer, but her sigh betrayed her desire. "I just put my lipstick on, and I think it looks better on me than you."

Matthew had to agree, the bright red lips that matched the cherries on her white A line dress made her look delicious enough to eat, but he needed to shower and clean himself up a bit to be suitable for their date. Chuckling to himself over the thought of it being a date, Matthew simply placed a seductive kiss behind her ear, and took himself off to the bathroom.

Using a garbage bag, Matthew taped the makeshift raincoat over his stupid ankle and sat in the shower chair and let the warm water distract him. It really had been the best week of his life. Seven days of complete and utter bliss. And tonight. Their first official date. He was stressed that they were just doing what they always did. Maybe he should have planned something better? More romantic? But Tuesday Pizza night was part of their tradition, and tonight was going erase all the damage that last week's drama had done.

Wrapping himself in a towel, Matthew cursed himself for forgetting his clothes when he came in. Still dripping slightly, after removing the plastic from his foot, he left the bathroom and hobbled towards the bedroom. The way Beth paused when she saw him made him feel bloody fantastic again. But it wasn't his face she was staring at. It was the soft towel Matthew had clung around his waist.

Beth had to remind herself to breathe. Standing there, still dripping with water, hair dishevelled and turned darker from the shower, Matthew looked like a photoshopped Mills and Boon cover. Man he was *hawt*! And just to think, all that was stopping her from seeing him, all of him, was that small towel. Then, he opened his mouth, "Like what you see baby? I can lose the towel anytime you want." Beth let out a chuckle that broke the tension in the air. Sexy as hell, and now that he knew the affect he was having on her, he was taking advantage of it.

Keeping her eyes on Matthew, Beth moved closer, picking up his clothes on the way around the bed. Handing them to him, Beth let her hand drift down his moist chest, finding his belly button. Tickling it, she kept walking and went to the kitchen to give him some privacy to get dressed. It was too much of a temptation to stay and watch him get dressed. She needed a cold drink after seeing him like that.

Making their way to the pizza place, they sat opposite each other in a small corner, as far away from their normal table as possible. Beth ordered for them, much to Matthews chagrin, and as they ate, they held hands and talked about the events for the rest of the week. At some point Matthew needed to go home. And at some point, Beth knew she needed to tell her parents. Pushing all the heavy stuff aside, Beth focussed on the gorgeous man in front of her, shared the pizza and coke, and let the rightness of it all sink in.

When they got home, Matthew stopped Beth on the doorstep. He wanted to do this first date properly. And yes, they were going inside together anyway, but kissing her goodnight on the doorstep seemed like such a natural thing to do. It was the perfect end to a lovely evening, where they had talked, laughed and playfully touched each other. Matthew had looked into her eyes and seen what he knew was inside him too. True love. Soppy, romantic, flowers and chocolates, never ending love that seemed so powerful, Matthew felt like he was literally glowing from the inside out.

Braking off the kiss, Matthew sighed and held Beth's hand as she unlocked the door and they entered the haven of home. The idea that they could lay together and have a little good night make out session made him grin from ear to ear. His ribs were still too sore to allow much more, but this was a marathon not a sprint and he was happy to be pacing himself.

As the weeks went on, the complete passion Matthew felt for Beth only grew. He really didn't know how much longer they could go on without taking it to the next level. They had explored a lot of each other's bodies so far, but never south of the waist and this was the longest time Matthew had gone without a release for at least 3 years now. Despite the fact he was yearning for her, he was far from bored. But Matthew got the feeling Beth was still holding back a little.

She wouldn't undress in front of him, making sure her incredible body was hidden from him and he longed to get a glimpse of her naked skin. He had basically memorised her breasts through Braille, the hardness of her nipples excited him, as she clearly liked his touch. Her smooth neck, and that soft spot behind her ears drove him mad. He felt overwhelmingly attracted to her and she was so cheeky!

When she left the apartment this morning before him, Beth had squeezed his ass, kissed him on the cheek and whispered, "love your cheeks" before rushing out the door. The cheeky banter they had always had continued much to Matthew's delight. Only now, kitten played back. Beth challenged him mentally, stimulated him sexually and turned his heart to mush emotionally. He couldn't believe they had wasted so much time pretending they weren't in love.

Cleaning up the kitchen before he left, Matthew glanced at the bed they shared. five weeks straight he had slept there, but the best part was the wake up. The bed hair and morning breath, the sleep in her eyes, the lines on her face where she had slept on the pillow. Every part of it amazed him. And that first kiss to start the day. The kind of thing poetry was written about. Matthew knew he had turned from a promiscuous boy, to a completely devoted, loved up mush almost overnight. And he had never felt better.

Heading to the doctor, Matthew prayed for good news about his ankle. His ribs, although no longer bruised on the outside, ached a little, but he was desperate to get the moon boot off his foot. It was a hit to his masculinity when he still needed his girlfriend's help to do basic things. Girlfriend. No longer feeling disgusted at the term, he said it with glee. Tonight, they were going to a footy catch up together.

The team had called him during the week, inviting him. They had only had two more warm up games since his collision, and his mate had sorted his car out, but Matthew had stayed away from the games. He was a competitive bastard, and not playing was torture. Funnily enough, Beth missed one game, but went to the last one because she missed the boys too much. He wasn't jealous – much, but when she came home with mud on her knees and her hair all scruffy from being on the field, Matthew had nearly ripped her clothes off and ignored the awkward moon boot situation.

This trip to the pub tonight, was the first social event they were attending as an official couple. They hadn't kept it a secret, but they also hadn't wanted to share each other with anyone right now. The time together, home and cosy had been too tempting. It was exciting. The team would all know she was his. And it was adorable since they had sent Bethany a separate text inviting her tonight. It made him proud that his mates thought so fondly about her too. She was an integral part of his whole life and it made him fucking ecstatic.

CHAPTER 28

Beth had an OK day at Uni. It did seem to drag though. She was nervous about the night. She wasn't worried the team wouldn't accept her. She was worried it would change her position on the team. Would they treat her different? Would they stop flirting with her? Would they think of her as a 'girl' now and not let her in the change rooms? She didn't want anything to change that way.

With a sigh, Beth finished her last class, and packed up. She had seen Jo around campus, but never talked to her. Bethany felt bad about that, she really did. But how do you start a conversation with someone after fallout like that night? 'Hi, great to see you, sorry, the boy you liked, well we are together now, and your cousin is a douche?' – um, NO, Beth thought to herself.

Matthew wasn't home when Bethany dumped her things on the kitchen table and looked around. She loved how he always did little things around the apartment when she wasn't there. Beth had made the bed before she left, but her dirty dishes were clean and dried in the drainer. The bench was wiped clean and the chairs all pushed in neatly to the table just as she liked them.

She had practically lived with Matthew for years now, so it shouldn't have been a surprise how thoughtful he was. In fact, the full time living arrangements had been a breeze. They already knew each other's annoying habits, and they moved in harmony around the kitchen, making dinner together most nights and never argued about what to watch on TV. The only fights so far had been about the toilet seat, but Beth figured that was an age-old argument many couples had.

The best thing about dating her best friend? He knew all her ugly sides and loved her anyway. They skipped all the uneasy, getting to know you bullshit and moved straight into the good stuff. It still seemed too good to be real. And Beth knew it wasn't going to be long until they knew each other in more intimate ways. That was another thing that scared the shit out of Beth. The moment was coming when he would see her body fully. Yes, he liked what he saw so far, but Beth still felt uneasy about what was to come.

Unsure what to wear to the pub, Beth headed for the shower to try and relax her tense shoulders. Her niggling self-doubt was taking its toll on her. She had even talked to her mum about it. But in the end, it was Beth's problem alone, and her mum was right. She couldn't ever truly love someone else until she loved herself. Another sigh left her lips as she turned the water off and reached for her towel.

Not finding it where she left it Beth opened the shower screen to look for it, only to see Matthew leaning against the door frame with an intense gaze in his eyes. Beth struggled to cover herself and shouted at Matthew to hand her a towel. But he didn't move. Matthew simply roamed his gaze from her face downwards over her naked breasts and lower still. Beth shivered under his gaze, partly from the water turning cold on her wet skin, and partly due to the scrutiny she was under.

"Move your hands baby, I need to see all of you." Matthew whispered. Beth was frozen to the spot. When she didn't move, Matthew held the towel out wide enticing her with its warmth. "If you want the towel Bethy, you need to come and get it. But I'm kinda hoping you don't want it, because I am in heaven." Matthew said slowly as a smile crept to his lips.

Beth's worst nightmare had come true. Here she stood, naked in front of the one person that mattered the most. The one person she desperately wanted to want her. The dodgy lighting in the bathroom was not kind to her skin, and she was very conscious of the untrimmed bikini line sticking out the sides where her hand covered. Desperately looking around the room for something to cover herself, Beth was almost hysterical with anxiety.

Placing a warm hand on her shoulder, Beth hadn't noticed Matthew approach. He turned her around, facing him and swept a hand down her neck, across her shoulder and down to her hips. The other hand stayed on her shoulder, gently making circles and goose bumps on her skin. Lowering his gaze from her eyes to her lips, Matthew trembled himself as he closed the distance and kissed Beth. But he would not get consumed in this kiss. There was more to see and do, and Matthew intended to enjoy this moment and make Beth know true pleasure for the first time.

Stepping back from his girl, Matthew lowered his gaze to her chest. Her perfect round breasts and oh so hard nipples made Matthew gasp for breath. "You literally take my breath away" Matthew said, breaking the silence. Beth felt a sob rising in her chest. How can he mean it? Here she was, in front of him, and he hadn't run. In fact, he had possessed her, come after her. As Matthew bent down and placed his mouth over hers again, Beth no longer felt cold. In fact, she was starting to warm up from the inside out.

Once again breaking the kiss, Matthew moved his mouth downwards, trailing kisses down her neck, shoulder and oh so gently over her left breast. Sucking her nipple in, Matthew relished the sharp intake of breath from his girl, and he made his way to the next supple breast. His next move, brought him to his knees, as he kissed down Beth's body, paying particular attention to her adorable belly button. She giggled as he kissed it again, and the sound of her laugh made him the proudest guy in the world.

Beth's worried gasp then put a halt to proceedings, as she pulled him to his feet. "Your ankle Matthew, you should not be doing that."

"Aww baby, I was exactly where I wanted to be, look, no cast!"

Matthew declared, sporting an intense looking taped foot. "I have to go back tomorrow for x-rays, but they let me have the night off as long as I promised to be good. And baby, I fully intend to be good for you." Matthew said cheekily as he not so subtly checked out her naked body. "Oh, baby, you are everything to me, and I refuse to let you cover yourself up anymore."

CHAPTER 29

Holding her hand, Matthew led Beth towards the bedroom, his limp hardly noticeable, his erection not so subtle. Walking was only difficult because of the bulge in his pants not the tape on his foot. Removing his own shirt, Beth gasped again as she noticed his taped ribs. Assuring her they didn't hurt, it was just a precaution, Matthew guided Beth to lay on the bed. And what a sight she made. Matthew thought he was going to come just looking at her. He especially liked the slightly trimmed, but not overly groomed patch of hair covering her privates.

Laying down next to her, Matthew took his time, running his fingers over every inch of Beth skin, stroking up over her breasts, and downwards towards her warm middle. As his hands started to skim her sensitive inner leg, and explore the curves of her thighs, Beth began to relax. The scared-shocked expression on her face had turned to growing desire. She placed her hands on Matthews ripped chest and made her own moves south. Not holding it together well, Matthew placed a probing kiss to her lips, forcing his way inside her mouth, while still massaging the inside of her thigh. Moving his fingers with skill, Matthew moaned in pleasure as he felt the warmth of her insides, and the thrust of her body towards his.

Bethany was out of her mind with lust. Matthew was amazing with his hands as they penetrated her, and found the right spot, sending those tingles up her body. But she knew his clever hands were not enough. She wanted all of him. Trying to stay focused was difficult as Matthew pleasured her with kisses and his fingers, but Beth was determined. Moving her hands to his jeans, Beth easily undid the button, and boldly unzipped his fly. Beth grazed his erection with the back of her hand as she pulled the zip down, and Matthew had to come up for air. "You have no idea how good that feels baby" he croaked, before attaching himself to her neck.

Happy that she seemed to be doing the right thing, Beth pulled away from Matthew so she could remove his jeans. No one ever told her how hard it would be to get undressed in the middle of it. You literally had to stop what you were doing to get to the good part. But when she stepped back, her reward was clear. His amazing body, toned, and hard in all the right places, as he looked at her in hunger. "I am hoping you like what you see baby, because the view I have is pretty awesome."

Beth blushed at the compliment. She was still too nervous for words. But suddenly her nakedness didn't seem to worry her. There was no mistaking how Matthew felt about her body. The evidence of his attraction was right in front of her, giving her confidence and a little bit of sass. Starting at his toes, Beth rubbed her hands softly up his legs, over his knees and across his muscular thighs. Reaching his groin, Beth gently rubbed him, and felt a thrill go through her at his reaction.

But it wasn't enough. She was ready to give all of herself to him, and take everything from him. Slipping her hands into the waistband of his nicely fitting underwear, Beth teased him with small movements, and playful tickles. Before she had the chance to completely undress him, Matthew sprung up from the bed and kissed her senseless. Pulling each other close, Beth could feel his hardness, his size and his passion. It was her turn to drop to her knees, and as she slid down his body, she slowly removed his pants, careful not to decapitate little Matthew as she did so.

Beth's first thought was that it looked too big to possibly fit. She wasn't an expert, this was her first time, but how could all of that feel good inside her. Maybe they had found the one way they weren't compatible? She had never heard anyone say they couldn't fit it inside them. Was that something people talked about she wondered. Seeing her hesitation, Matthew appeared to be reading her mind. Holding her to him, Matthew said quietly "I am worried it will hurt you the first-time baby. I think it seems so unfair that something so magical could even hurt you a little. So we don't have to go any further now OK?".

Beth stared at her boyfriend. His words, his true thoughtfulness for how it would feel for her, made her want him even more. She didn't answer. Beth simply laid down on the bed, and patted the space next to her. Matthew didn't take his eyes off her as he followed her lead. As Beth leaned over and kissed him, Matthew reached for her body and pulled them together. With his hands skimming the side of her waist and gently feeling her ass, Matthew had never been this hot for a girl in his life. But he would put on the brakes if she needed to.

Beth's tongue moving over his, obliviated any further coherent thoughts, as they both succumbed to the pleasure and passion. The way Beth was grinding against him drove him wild, as he thrust his hands into her hair, pulling her mouth closer. But none of it was enough. Returning his fingers to her warm, delicate parts, Matthew revelled in the soft, silky feel of her, and the moans of pleasure she let out. With his fingers inside her, Matthew dropped his head to suck on her nipples once again, and he knew she was on the edge of euphoria. As she let out a pleasurable moan, Matthew removed his fingers, found the small packet that he had placed in the bedside drawer this morning, and rolled the protection on.

Looking down at her body, before moving over her, Matthew could feel the heat from her skin and demanded another sweet kiss from his girl. As they joined together for the first time, Matthew kept looking into those dreamy eyes, and braced for the initial pain of a virginity lost. Beth let out a startled gasp, but stopped Matthew from pulling out.

The pain was sharp, but as Matthew began to move inside her, Beth focused on the parts of them that were touching. His tight bum and strong leg muscles aiding his movements and the unbelievable feeling as he found a rhythm that intensified quickly. Beth could feel the strong muscles in his back and as he kissed her again, the feeling of intense warmth filled her, blocking out the initial pain. With the sweat growing on their bodies, and the rush of Matthew's orgasm filling her senses, Beth let herself fall into bliss.

CHAPTER 30

Letting their breathing slow to normal pace, Matthew and Beth looked into each other's eyes. The flush of Beth's cheeks, the dishevelled mess of her hair and the redness of her swollen lips made Matthew blink back tears. She was perfect for him. And what had just happened, was pure joy. Wary of his weight on top of her, Matthew pulled out of Beth and sat up to deal with the condom. To his surprise, Beth sat up too, watching him. Now it was his turn to blush. She watched as he went out of the room, and couldn't help but admire the view of his naked ass.

When Matthew returned, Beth was curious what he had done with it. "So, what happens with those once you are done?" Beth asked. Smiling at her innocent question, Matthew returned to the space next to her and pulled her into a cuddle. Which surprised the shit out of him, because he had never cuddled after sex before.

"I wrapped it up in toilet paper and put it in the bin." He said quietly, running his fingers through her hair.

"Oh, OK. I always wondered what that would be like. So, is there a difference with how it feels with the condom on, or off? It seemed OK to me, but is it the same for you? I mean, they have so many different kinds in the pharmacy, how can we be sure that it is ok for you? It's not like you can ask the pharmacist, right? That would be weird…" Beth rambled quickly until Matthew cut her off with a finger to her lips.

"Beth baby, slow down. I'm glad you have questions but take a breather." Matthew laughed. "Officially the coolest girl ever BTW's. The disposal of a condom is not actually the kind of thing I have ever discussed with anyone. No, don't frown baby, that's a good thing. I love that we can say exactly what we want to each other. But let me get this straight. Are you are asking if the condom felt OK? As in, there was a chance that I didn't enjoy myself?" Matthew asked in disbelief.

"Umm, yeah. I mean, I want to know everything about it, and I'm sure I will get better at it, but it stopped so suddenly I kind of thought I did something that you know, didn't feel good for you. And I want you to tell me OK? I want to…" Beth's next words were stifled by Matthew's mouth.

A slow, passionate kiss that warmed her inside again and had them scrambling back on the bed to hold each other tightly. Caressing her mouth with his, Matthew wanted his actions to speak louder than his words. How could she think he didn't enjoy himself? Running his tongue over her bottom lip, Matthew pulled back from his girl. "You are amazing. Baby, the reason it stopped so quickly was my fault. Normally I take a little longer to, you know, but Beth, you drive me so wild I literally couldn't control myself. My biggest worry is that it hurt you too much. But I'm guessing it felt OK, because that little moan you gave, blew my world away."

"Oh, alright then, the only advice my Mum could give me was to relax, and to talk and be honest with you. She said that's where most people go wrong, they don't talk about what they like and don't like." Beth mumbled shyly.

"Oh my god, your Mum knows we are having sex? Or thinking about having sex. That means your Dad knows." Matthew said anxiously.

"Relax, I think they would gather that would happen. We are adults. And you know I tell my Mum everything." Beth said as she sat up cross legged on the bed and faced Matthew. "So, my question about the condom? You think that was silly? Because I would like to know."

"Ha, OK" Matthew said sitting up, propping himself on the head board. "I honestly couldn't say. I have never had sex without a condom.

And never had a conversation about condoms other than the Sex Ed discussions at school. Never wanted any chance of little Matthew's around. There has only been one girl that I would ever consider having kids with, and she is in this room with me."

A beautiful smile broke out on Beth's face. She felt the same. The idea of someone else ever touching her was repulsive. "I can't believe we just had sex!" Beth said laughing.

Matthew couldn't hold back his own laughter. He would never have imagined a conversation like this. He knew she was nervous, but how cute was she? Looking at the clock, Matthew had an idea. He really was brilliant sometimes. "Baby girl, we need to get going soon. But I think I owe you another shower. Come with me, and I will wash your hair for you."

The gleam in Beth's eyes told him she liked that idea. Now she was over her shyness about her body, he might have to invent a house rule that she stay naked all day. But that wouldn't be too productive to their lives he guessed. Leading Beth into the shower, he took his time washing her body thoroughly, and massaging the conditioner into her hair. And when Beth slid her hands over his chest and lower, Matthew couldn't believe how quickly he was ready to go again. But that would have to wait. He was eager to take his girl out tonight. A point of pride for him, to be actually telling everyone they were together. He even changed his Facebook status today, which was surprising since he never used the thing. Beth did though, so he was wondering when she would see it.

Drying off took a bit longer than usual, as they kept stopping to kiss and then had to break themselves apart to get dressed. Beth wore a beautiful soft pink shirt that pulled tightly across her perfect chest, and some dark jeans that gave Matthew a very nice view of her ass. When she went to put makeup on, Matthew stopped her. She didn't need it. Like she was, hair still damp, drying in soft waves, rosy cheeks from the mischief they had been up to and a pink flower in her hair, her beauty was natural. And when Matthew told her that, she blushed even more, making him smile.

Insisting on picking out his shirt, Beth was undecided what she wanted to see him in. Walking around like he was right now, in just his underwear, was kind of awesome. Settling on a white long sleeve shirt, Beth ogled him as he stepped into his jeans. He was like a freakin pin up model! Helping him with his shirt, Beth did each button up slowly, never taking her eyes off his green ones. The smirk on his lips told her that he was enjoying the moment as much as she was. Rolling his sleeves up for him, Beth couldn't decide what had been sexier. The heated moments in the shower, or the intense atmosphere as she dressed him.

CHAPTER 31

Making their way to the pub, Matthew and Beth found themselves giggling most of the way. But Matthew could tell Beth had something on her mind. "What you thinking about Bethy?" He said, sliding his hand up her thigh as she drove. Sucking in a breath, Beth turned briefly and smiled a radiant smile.

"Just wondering how everyone will take it now that we are, you know, dating. I don't want anything to change with all the boys. They have always treated me like one of the gang, like they had forgotten I was actually a girl. I hope that part stays the same." Beth admitted.

"Baby, you think they don't see you as a girl? Do you know how many of those boys I have had to set straight when they talked about your sexy ass or your perfect tits? Trust me, they know you are a girl!" Matthew chuckled.

Beth was a little shocked to hear that. But silently pleased. And when Matthew added "I am fairly certain if it wasn't made perfectly clear to those horny bastards that you were hands off, you would have had them lined up to date. I am going to enjoy this." Matthew said as Beth felt her grin widen.

"So who told them I was hands off Hue? Coach?" Beth questioned.

"Ha, Coach doesn't want to lose you, that's for sure. But seriously? You think all these years I would let you hang around those hooligans without making it clear that you were off limits? I have loved you my whole life Baby, even before I knew I did." Matthew stated.

Letting that information set in, Beth and Matthew held hands the rest of the way in a comfortable silence. They parked and Beth helped Matthew out of the car despite the absence of his cast. The little action they had earlier had been amazing, but Beth could tell Matthew was not as 'fine' as he claimed to be. She just let the macho stuff go and preserved the poor boy's dignity.

As they reached the door, Matthew pulled Beth close and kissed her. "I love you so much Beth, and I am so fucking proud to be walking in with you now."

They entered the bar hand in hand and quickly found the team. It wasn't hard to find them despite the noisy bar. They were all huge and rowdy. Seeing Matthew and Beth approach, the guys let out cheer and ordered drinks. No one seemed overly bothered by the fact they were holding hands. Beth realised it was because they often did that, even before all the fun stuff.

When Matthew let go of her hand, and went to collect their drinks, Beth looked around the crowed room. She wasn't sure what made her do it, but as she turned back to her group her gaze landed on a familiar but unwanted figure. Corey approached Beth from around a corner of the bar he was inhabiting with a group of his own friends. Beth cursed under her breath, as she tried to calculate the chances of them being in the same bar and the same time.

"Hello there Bethany, you are looking mighty fine tonight."

"Fuck off Corey you sleaze bag, run back to your friends. I'm guessing they don't know what a tosser you are?" Beth spat back at him.

Clearly infuriated, Corey snapped his hand forward and grasped Beth's arm. As he increased the pressure, Beth struggled to get away from his cement grip. "Who do you think you are, you crazy cow? I wasted so much time trying to get in your pants, and what did you expect. Your friend is hot. You can't possibly imagine someone as good looking as me would pass up that opportunity." Corey said louder than necessary.

As Beth continued to struggle, a large warm hand landed on her shoulder, while the matching hand landed on Corey's wrist. Beth looked up into the eyes of Max, as he forced Corey to release his hold on Beth. "Excuse me dude, but that is my girl, so get your hands off her now, before I break every bone in your body." Max growled in a deep voice. Beth found herself holding back a giggle.

"Yeah right, you really think you would bash me for this girl?" Corey shouted, and for his answer, Max stepped into his personal space and glared at him. As Corey looked around for help, all he found was more buff, angry bodies, as the team, Beth's team, stood behind Max, and looked menacing. And then, Matthew wrapped his arms around Beth's waist and pulled her against his hard chest.

Whispering into Beth's ear Matthew said, "I can't leave you alone for one minute can I baby? You have men at your feet!" Beth giggled harder at that statement, relieving some of the tension she had been feeling, but drawing Corey's attention once again.

"Seems like you get around then Beth, good thing I didn't touch you, who knows what I would have caught? Who would really want you anyway?" Corey said smugly as he stepped back from the wall of body guards surrounding Beth.

"I want her" came the call, then another, "She is my girl". "Beth is my one and only" came another as the bar filled with the voices of the team, all claiming her as theirs. It brought tears to Beth's eyes and a scowl to Corey's. As he retreated, walking backwards, his eyes fixed on the crowd, Beth thought she heard him say something but all she could make out was "Not worth it."

Taking a deep breath, Beth turned around and clung to Matthew, as the team gathered closer around them. Max stepped closer and said cheerfully, "Well that was fun! I am a little disappointed the dick finally got smart and left you alone though, cos he needed a broken nose for sure." With that, the team laughed and returned to their earlier positions with their drinks.

Beth stayed with a vice grip around Matthew. She slowly calmed her racing heart and willed her eyes to not betray her. Matthew, sensing her tears, pulled her back enough to be able to see her face. Using his thumb to wipe away the few stray tears that had managed to escape, Matthew bent down and kissed under each eye, before planting a firm and lingering kiss to Beth's lips. He would never get tired of this, and in that moment, when she needed comfort, he was very happy to be the one to give it. As the kiss continued, Matthew heard whistles and claps that drew his attention away from his girlfriend.

Turning, Beth and Matthew saw the team, watching and cheering. Matthew smiled wide and then bowed low, eliciting further hoots and laughter. Pulling Beth along towards the bar, someone handed Matthew a drink and slapped him on the back. Next, Beth was provided a beverage, and they fielded questions about how long they had been together. The general consensus was that everyone knew it would happen eventually. And although there were many of his mates that pleaded with Beth to dump Matthew and choose them instead, he could tell they were all happy with the outcome.

Beth snapped endless photos with the boys during the night, clearly putting the drama behind her. When Bethany returned to Matthews side for a selfie, wanting to post the photos to Facebook, Matthew could tell the moment Beth had noticed his status update. Her squeal of delight made Matthew chuckle to himself and the kiss she laid on his mouth told him she approved of the public notice. Matthew was relieved. Now that they were publicly a couple, he could relax in the knowledge that the world knew she was his. And that was worth more than a million dollars.

EPILOGUE

Christmas was always a nice time for Matthew at the Holden's house. The scent of vanilla from the kitchen and the ever-present carols playing softly in the background made him feel eight years old again. But this Christmas was going to be even better. Having taken Vince aside for a private chat, the men emerged from the shed smiling and shaking hands.

Beth was in the kitchen with her mum when she noticed them laughing. "What are you two up too?" Beth asked as they came back into the house.

"Your Dad just wanted to show me his new tools. Very nice Mrs H, you spoilt the big guy." Matthew said, brushing a kiss on Beth's cheek and then her mum's.

Handing plates and cutlery to the men, Beth shooed them off to set the table for lunch. They had spent the night apart, each choosing to stay with their family for the Christmas day wake up. But Beth was glad Matthew had finally arrived. They had seen each other every day since the first night they kissed.

Matthew had always claimed that Beth was the one saving him. But in Beth's mind, Matthew saved her from herself. After lunch, Matthew suggested they go for a walk and her parents insisted they leave the dishes and go. Strolling hand in hand, they walked down the familiar streets and made their way towards the school. The place they met Beth mused to herself.

Slipping in the old gate that had never locked properly, Matthew led Beth over to the swing and insisted she sit so he could push her. She giggled and flung her legs up in the air making herself go higher until she jumped off and landed with a thud in the sand. Still laughing, Beth looked around for Matthew. He was across the old playground, in his hand, a paper aeroplane ready to fly.

Letting it go, Matthew's aim was perfect and it landed just a step away from Beth's feet. As she bent down to retrieve it, she saw Matthew approach smiling. Curious, Beth opened the note, and the two words she read stopped her heart. Looking up from the note, Beth's eyes found Matthews' as he knelt down on one knee in front of her. Holding the most beautiful Amethyst ring, Matthew kept his eyes on Beth.

Not at all what Beth was expecting, she felt tears in her eyes as she processed the shock. He was asking me to marry him? "I, ah, I need to sit down" Beth said in a daze.

Matthew helped her to the bench and took her hands in his. "I know it is fast Beth. But it isn't really. We have known each other our whole lives. I talked to your Dad. I, ah, I, asked his permission and all. He is really happy for us. He told me I was the only bloke he could imagine you being with and that he agreed that we would be wasting our time with a long engagement."

Hearing that made Beth cry even harder and Matthew started to feel worried. "Please tell me this is a good cry and not a bad cry Bethy, cos you are kind of freaking me out here." Matthew said nervously.

Hearing that, Beth realised she hadn't answered him. Of course, in her mind, she had said yes, the second she read the short 'Marry me?' on the paper. Had she really forgotten to say yes out loud? The poor guy! Pulling herself together, Beth wiped her eyes and looked back at her wonderful friend. It had been six months of exploration, laughter and the most amazing sex, but the best part had been the enduring friendship they had maintained. Closing her eyes to steady her nerves, Beth placed a hand on Matthews handsome face, and whispered, "yes".

He wanted to shout, 'Thank fuck for that!' but Matthew settled for a shaky laugh as he slipped the ring on her finger. My fiancé he thought. And then, because he wanted to hear the sound of it, he said it out loud. "My fiancé".

Bethany giggled and plastered a kiss on his lips. They walked home arm in arm, with Beth holding her adorned finger out in front of them the whole way. Sharing the news with her parents was another tearful exchange, the love in the small house filling their hearts and their heads. They were about to cheers with a bottle of pink champagne when there was a knock on the door.

Practically floating to answer it, Beth opened the door wide with a smile that faulted when she saw who it was. Lori stood before her, perfectly dressed and looking like a catwalk model. She hadn't seen the girl since that night and she wasn't really in the mood to see her now. It was Christmas day she conceded, they were occupying the same small space in Cloverdale, it did seem inevitable.

"Can we talk?" Lori said, keeping her eyes focused on Beth.

"Sure, why not, come in." Beth led Lori through to her old bedroom, wanting to keep this as low key and private as possible.

Closing the door, Beth began to speak but Lori cut her off. "Listen, I need you to listen to me OK? I understand you have been avoiding me, but I beg you to just give me a few minutes to talk, please?"

Nodding, Beth sat at her old but sturdy desk, while Lori took the bed.

"Sounds like you guys are celebrating out there hey? Can I guess what this is about? I was kind of hoping you said yes when Matthew asked you to marry him?"

Absolutely flabbergasted, Beth just nodded her head once again and sat in silent confusion.

"Matthew told me, that's how I know. He and I have been texting. Nothing like that, so don't worry, it's just that, I needed to know if you were OK, and if you two had finally got together. It was killing me not knowing that, and I thought at least if you were together, then it was all worth it even if I did lose you over it."

"What do you mean, it was all worth it? What the hell are you talking about Lori?" Beth spoke for the first time since their arrival in the room.

"See, this is where it gets a bit tricky. I want to be honest with you and tell you, that night, I had no intention of flirting with that dickwad. All I wanted to do was come down and meet him and maybe help you to realise that you were better off with your crush boy. And then that ridiculous sleaze bag started making eyes at me, with you standing right there. I didn't plan it I swear. But I thought if you could see what a loser he was, you would be able to focus on Matthew better. And I knew, from talking with Josh, that Matthew felt the same way about you. But you are both so bloody self-righteous and stubborn, we felt you needed a push to get it together."

"You did it on purpose? You knew Matthew liked me? I can't wrap my head around that Lori, I really can't." Beth said, beginning to pace the small room. "And what do you mean you knew from Josh. Since when did any of this happen? I am so bloody confused right now I don't know what to say."

"Beth listen, I will explain everything later, I just wanted to get a chance to see you. Matthew sent me a text when you were on your way home from your walk so I knew when you were here. He thought you would be in a better mood after he proposed so that would be the best time to come over."

"He planned all of this? The proposal, you coming over and everything?" Beth squeaked in shock as she fell to her knees.

"He did. He really has been amazing Beth. He rang me the day after you two got together and said he wanted to talk. He has been keeping me up to date with how you are and he even asked my opinion about the ring. I think it's perfect for you by the way." Lori said, lowering herself to the floor with Beth.

"I feel so silly. Matthew has said this whole time that I needed to talk to you. I couldn't bare to think about it anymore. I wanted to just stay in our happiness bubble and forget about how much you hurt me. But he's right. I can't say I am completely over what happened, but I do understand your intentions." Beth cried as she wrapped her arms around Lori.

"We can work on trusting each other again Beth, if you want to? I don't want to lose you. But I respect that you need time." Lori said between sobs. After the crying had stopped from both girls, Beth had another question she had to ask. "Where have you been staying Lori? I feel like such a shit head for not even knowing that."

Lori smiled, and took a deep breath. "Well, about that. I have been staying with a friend. A male friend and up until three days ago it was strictly PG. But, something happened and I actually think I might want to keep him around for a while."

A knock on the bedroom door made the girls jump and scream. Then they laughed at their reaction before calling in unison "YES?"

"Babe, my brother is here and he wanted to say congrats and all that. Are you girls done in there yet?" Matthew called through the still closed door.

Beth gasped, looking to Lori as understanding dawned on her. "Are you telling me that you and Josh…"

"Yes!" Lori squealed and the girls laughed and hugged again. Finally emerging from the bedroom, Beth wrapped her arms around Josh and felt like a hole had been filled. Her friend was happy, her fiancé was the sexiest man on earth, and the people she loved most in the world were standing in the small lounge room of her childhood home.

Handing out more glasses of champagne, the Holden's welcomed everyone into their home and Beth felt herself blush at the attention. She would have to get used to it if she was going to be a bride. She could hardly believe it. A bride! A wedding. And as she surveyed the room in front of her, she smiled to herself, as she thought, wow, was Matthew going to look good in a tux or what?

The End…or the beginning?

Printed in the United States
By Bookmasters